THE ODD FELLOWS

Visit us at www.boldstrokesbooks.com

THE ODD FELLOWS

by

Guillermo Luna

A Division of Bold Strokes Books

2013

THE ODD FELLOWS
© 2013 By Guillermo Luna. All Rights Reserved.

ISBN 13: 978-1-60282-969-5

This Trade Paperback Original Is Published By
Bold Strokes Books, Inc.
P.O. Box 249
Valley Falls, NY 12185

First Edition: December 2013

Images on pgs. 1, 7, 15, 35, 57, 71, 91, 113, 133, 169, 197 are taken from The Odd-Fellows Manual by Rev. Aaron B. Grosh (Philadelphia: H. C. Peck & Theo. Bliss, 1852).

Credits
Editors: Greg Herren and Stacia Seaman
Production Design: Stacia Seaman
Cover Design by Sheri (graphicartist2020@hotmail.com)

For all the odd fellows around the world.

I.

JOAQUIN MORENO'S JOURNAL: THE DEAD BODY

Mark Crowden always says people shouldn't go shopping for clothes when they're sleepy because they'll make bad fashion choices. As I stood in Mark's dining room—looking at a yellow, green, and red piñata that was supposedly a depiction of El Chupacabras—I wondered how sleepy and *drunk* he must have been to purchase it and then stumble home with this horror clutched to his chest.

"Well," I said, "you're the only person I know who has an El Chupacabras piñata. I wouldn't have it in my home but *I do like it*. I guess we just decorate differently. I like fine antiques from the end of the nineteenth century, and you like cheap Mexican stuff."

Mark took his big beefy index finger, the one on his

right hand, and poked me in the forehead. "You're right. *Me gusta.*"

It's all due to the "resort." The uncertainty over the purchase of the structure, Cascada, has created a continuous cloud of stress over him. He is benevolent and amusing, but because of his dealings with Mexican officials he has become a snarling, husky dandy in brown leather sandals. Every one of his negative traits has been swirled together to produce a tornado of snarky comments directed at *todos en el mundo* and specifically, his immediate brotherhood.

I'm partially to blame.

He used my own words against me. Maybe if I had been more piñata supportive he would have responded in a more civilized manner. It's that, combined with the land deal and those *horrid* Mexican officials holding up the sale. All of this is their fault.

I will admit finding the dead body on the property before the deal closed was alarming. Yet one dead body shouldn't prevent us from buying the property. The land agent, a Mr. De La Santos, said the dead woman was in her thirties. If I remember his letter correctly, he stated she was an indigenous woman from the hills outside of San Felipe, who was called Loca Rosa. "The *policía* stated that she would wander the streets dressed in layers upon layers of clothing."

According to the authorities she didn't care what her clothing looked like, but these men couldn't have been more wrong.

I was told she was fond of long, full skirts. She would wear a plaid skirt over a green skirt over a striped skirt over a black skirt and on and on, so her lower half ballooned out as if she were wearing a hoop skirt from the Civil War era. A bolero jacket over a sweater over a shirt would be worn on top. She finished it all off with a bizarre hat concoction that included plastic flowers piled high upon the top and plastic fruit suspended from the brim with the aid of fishing wire.

Señor De La Santos said he would smile at her because she reminded him of a Christmas tree in her "getup." In a phone conversation he said whenever he would see her, he shook his head out of both wonder and bewilderment. Loca Rosa, according to Señor De La Santos, "dressed like no one else."

She kept her most prized possessions—a Bible, a plastic rosary, some mangos and oranges, and a cache of newspapers—in a small two-wheeled cart she dragged behind herself. The *policía* claimed that when she was hungry she would squat down next to the street and gnaw on oranges and mangos, eating the skin as well as the pulp. The juice from the fruit would drip down her chin, and she would not wipe it with a napkin or even her sleeve. While Mark said he could excuse, understand, and even (at times) encourage eccentric dressing habits, he couldn't forgive poor table manners. The poor thing may have been crazy and hungry, he said, but she should at least exhibit some proper etiquette while eating.

"It doesn't seem too much to ask even of the insane."

Mr. De La Santos's letter contained other elements, too, but most of them seemed unbelievable. It's the twenty-first century; superstition and third-world folklore are so twentieth century—so why even bring them into the mix? Yet various officials implied possibilities that led me to an uneasiness I consciously choose not to pursue. De La Santos claimed the body was nude and looked mummified when it was found.

"It was as if *la mujer* was a hundred, not thirty."

I do not believe him when he says the woman's body looked mummified. That could only happen if the body had been out in the sun for days or weeks, which seems unlikely. The coyotes that call the region home would have consumed the body long before the mummification process had taken place, and according to the *policía* the body was intact and contained only one animal's bite marks. I have come to the conclusion that Mr. De La Santos does not want to sell us the property and must have another buyer, yet Don Humberto has assured us by post that he is still interested in seeing the sale go through.

What is puzzling is that the *policía* report that Loca Rosa appeared to be making a daily pilgrimage to the structure we're attempting to purchase. She would travel to the location every day and chant in some indecipherable tongue for hours. No one who heard her knew what language she was speaking, but all agreed that it was a language, just not Spanish. Numerous people reported that she would chant while looking at the sky, and she would twirl. Yes, twirl. Some observers state that she appeared to be jumping while she twirled, but the prevalent and dominant movement seemed to be twirling. I can't think of any reason for an adult to twirl outside of dancing, so her chanting and twirling routine does seem, at the very least, odd. The location of the property we hope to acquire and where the body was found is approximately three miles outside of the San Felipe city limits. This means Loca Rosa would walk in that huge hoop-skirt contraption for three miles, past rocks and cactus, in ninety-degree heat. I personally feel the reason the poor thing was found nude was she finally became overheated and ripped off all her clothes. Whatever she was trying to hide no longer mattered; whatever protection the clothes gave her was no longer necessary.

Well, it should have ended right there with her death but, of course, it didn't. From what we've gathered, after the *policía* took photographs of Loca Rosa's body they left some intoxicated individual named "Enrique the guitar man" in charge of the body. Since Rosa didn't have any family, the *policía* gave Enrique a couple of pesos, and this was supposed to be the impetus for Enrique to wait with the body until the coroner arrived.

According to Mr. De La Santos, "Enrique the guitar man" is a local character who shows up after somebody has died to serenade the dead body. Kindness prevents me from labeling Enrique an opportunist.

Our friend Theodora said any man who devised a moneymaking scheme to milk grieving families out of pesos at the time of their greatest sorrow is an entrepreneur *and a ratfink.*

Enrique did wait. Unfortunately, Enrique consumed a pint of packy-packy gin while waiting and passed out before the coroner arrived. It was at this point that the body of Loca Rosa disappeared. No one is quite sure what happened. Enrique claims to have seen *un oso* before being struck on the back of the head, but in his state of sobriety no one takes his "oso" claim seriously. A bear in the middle of the desert? That doesn't make any sense, and besides, Enrique "wet himself" right before he passed out, so his memory and judgment are suspect. What is known for sure is that Loca Rosa's body was taken away by some animal. The large paw prints in the sand indicate this. There was one strange element that remains unexplained. Authorities found paw prints around the body but no paw prints to, or away from, the body.

II.
MARK CROWDEN'S BLOG: MEXICO

Let me tell you how it is—Joaquin is an idiot. If he wasn't contributing to the bankroll, I would dump his pansy ass. He would be *so* out of this deal. It's crystal clear Don Humberto still wants to sell us the property but it's De La Santos who's putting the kibosh on the sale. Santos must want a kickback. That won't happen. We'll race down there, talk to the Don, finalize the sale, and take possession. This Baja mansion, and all its fin-de-siècle beauty, is what we need. In my dreams I'm counting the dough while sitting in a big baroque chair, throwing my head back and laughing as my big man butt dances. I'll be the B&B kaiser of Mexico.

San Felipe is one of those foreign cities that most Americans don't know anything about. It's on the Gulf of California, approximately 119 miles east of Ensenada. The house is an eighteen-room Victorian in the Eastlake style. It has a clapboard exterior, which needs a good coat of paint, but because of the time required to paint it we won't do it. Instead we'll say we want it that way. We'll sell it as a green decision.

Theodora Russell agreed to be our third man, and she's certainly tough enough. In a street fight between her and Joaquin, I would put my money on the lady. She's agreed to forgo a paycheck until guests start checking in, but TR put it on the line when she told Joaquin and Markie that she has some money "saved up" *but* wasn't "flush" and didn't want to spend any of her own money on food or travel expenses. I told her I was "down with that" but I wouldn't pay for any hoochie-coochie products.

She said "Yeah" as she nodded and glared at me.

What's up with that?

We left Los Angeles at dusk and figured we would make it to the border in a couple of hours—longer, if we went the speed limit. Joaquin, the law abider, drove, so jeez Louise, it took forever to get to San Diego. He needs to stop being a little Latino safety twit. Take a chance, Joaquin. Drive like there's no *mañana*, Pepito. Besides, we brought along Joaquin's black-and-white French bulldog, Mr. Dangerous, for protection, and the world knows the ferocious reputation of le petit French bulldog.

The way I remember it was the way it was; a long three hours filled with cigarette smoke, arguments, screaming, the silent treatment, group singing, public urination, accusations, lies, occasionally the truth, and monotony. As our SUV crept to the border, pesky children approached and begged us to buy candy or gum. They wore Day of the Dead masks and were amazingly aggressive for children, but any charm they had was hidden behind their skeleton masks. I wondered why they weren't at home watching a crazy Spanish game show, but I guess there's no time for games when you're dead and have to work the streets. I didn't want Joaquin or Theodora to think I was one of those drunken, tenderhearted souls, so I made it translucently obvious that I only bought a pack of gum because the beggar kids didn't understand "no" in either English or Spanish. Plus, I could hear Joaquin repeatedly saying under his breath, "Relieve the distressed."

The Mexican official waved us through once he saw we were Americans, and the safety twit cautiously drove into the potholed streets of Tijuana. The streets were a mass of confusion *and* walking dead due to the Día de los Muertos celebration. We drove along one of the main drags, Revolución, looking for a place to stay overnight but had no luck. It was then that we pulled off onto a side street, which was a mistake.

A hectic haze of death encircled us. We were immediately surrounded by a mob of Mexican zombies, which prompted Joaquin to put on the brakes. There were probably fifty of them. This wasn't a crowd of idlers that we had inadvertently stumbled onto, 'cause they pawed at the vehicle and begged for money.

"Tienes un dólar, señor?"

The three of us stared out the windows, unsure what to do. Their death masks reflected onto the SUV's windows and doubled their numbers.

I smiled through clenched teeth and asked, "What's up with the tortilla eaters, Joaquin?"

"Tortilla eaters?"

He looked at me with a blank, expressionless face. "You're not being very helpful," he mumbled.

He turned away from me and stared at the beggars beyond

the glass divide. One of them had a nose slit and was leaving telltale nose marks on the glass. Eww.

I loudly said, "*My* people are from Dresden, so if we run into any spaetzel eaters, I'll know how to deal with them."

Theodora lit a cigarette, inhaled quickly, and spewed out a cloud of smoke before she spat out, "Stop your frickin' bickering, *bitches*."

Joaquin and I looked at each other. I mouthed the words "show people!" but he didn't respond. In this situation I had but one way to convey to Joaquin that everything was under control, that I would get us out of this situation, so I did what was required—I smiled a big smile that showed all my teeth. It makes me look like a cartoon bear. I glanced over my shoulder at Theodora.

"Hey! *THAT was crass.*"

Theodora exhaled a line of smoke in my direction. It hit me in the face and dissipated. She really uses those things like weapons.

The mob continued to paw at the vehicle and request money. *"Por favor, señor."*

"Please, señorita."

"Tienes un dólar?"

Then and there I told them we were going to do this my way; while it might be kind and generous to aid the efforts of the desolate and oppressed, Theodora and Joaquin were *forbidden* to open the doors or roll down any window no matter how sympathetic they might feel.

"*Focus, people.* We're safe as long as they stay outside and we stay inside."

With the determination of angry union workers the mob curled their hands into fists, lifted them above their heads, and began to pound the SUV.

Damn!

Annoyed, I ground my teeth into a smile.

In an attempt to make mob activity seem like it was part of my métier, I said, "I never expected the local color to be so angry."

I raised my eyebrows and nodded as I looked around at the mob outside the car.

From Theodora's lips emanated a statement that proved she was not an exemplar of our American epoch. She said without any hesitation, "If they start to get in, floor it!"

That tidbit went into my big head filing cabinet.

Mr. Dangerous was hiding under his blanket, but occasionally he stuck his snout out and barked. I speak in only the kindest terms, which isn't normal for me, when I say that dog is good for only one thing—being Joaquin's best friend and being a cutie, but criminy, we could have used a badass dog right then.

Our crusader came from around the corner, and unexpectedly, he resembled a big, fat egg. He turned on his light and siren and the whole incident was over. With a dispirited low energy that reflected the general malaise at the turn of events, the crowd began to disperse. They had to be upset that they had come close to making out like bandits and now they had nothing to show for it. How unfortunate for them. The officer drove up slowly and parked in front of our SUV. He sat in his vehicle and appraised all our provincial successfulness through his windshield before he got out and walked over to my window.

I rolled it down and was greeted by a *"buenas noches"* from Officer Martinez.

He said something about "getting ourselves in trouble" but it wasn't exactly clear because English wasn't his first language. Joaquin and Theodora were so relieved somebody had come to our aid that they nodded in agreement and thanked him in an effusive manner that is totally unbecoming in adults.

Those two would have agreed to anything at that moment, and regretfully they did when Officer Martinez said, "There must be chum way to cho your gratitude."

Joaquin tapped me on the arm and said, "Give him twenty bucks."

I turned to Joaquin with incredulity covering my face.

I asked, "Do you have twenty bucks?" but I said it in a drawn-out way that was designed to buy me a moment and prevent me from having to pry out my wallet.

Joaquin eagerly pulled out his wallet, fingered through it, and handed me a twenty.

I gave it to Officer Martinez and pointed at Joaquin. "It's from him."

Officer Martinez said, "And you?"

I concealed my disgust with a detached, repressed control that most men, myself included, are masters at. I smiled and said, *"No tienes dinero, señor."*

Fortunately for the Mexican Humpty Dumpty, Theodora was thrusting a twenty-dollar bill over my shoulder, which I relayed to him. Then there was silence. With the exception of mariachi music in the distance, complete and steady silence. I understood completely. His silence was an indication that Officer Martinez wanted more money from his American shakedown. I clasped my hands together and bowed. "Ah soy," I said.

I put on my bogus, charming face—the one with the insincere smile. With as much animation as I could marshal I said, *"Gracias!"*

I used big, wide eyes with the *thank you* and started moving my upper body from side to side in a jovial manner and ratcheted my arms up and down like I was beating a drum.

In a singsong I said, "Let's go, Joaquin!"

Joaquin looked at me as if my behavior was ridiculous-o, but the safety twit has known me long enough to know that sometimes it's best to do what I ask and not give Markie any lip. He started up the SUV, put it in reverse, and pulled around the officer's vehicle. As we drove away I could see Officer Martinez in my passenger side mirror, standing in the street, watching us. I expected him to follow but the big egg didn't.

Later that night we checked into a dive called Los Ojos Soñolientos, and the next morning I got up early and put on some plaid nerdy shorts (I can pull them off), a tank top, and leather sandals. I wore the shorts to show off my legs. I figured the people of Mexico needed some eye candy. Then I told Joaquin, who was still in bed, that I wanted to go down the street and see if I could find a sombrero and a poncho to wear so I wouldn't look so gringo.

Joaquin, with one eye open, gave me a confused look and said, "Are you taking Mr. Dangerous?"

Mr. Dangerous, who was at my feet, looked at his best friend and barked.

Joaquin limply waved good-bye before he rolled over to fall asleep again. As his gringo amigo, I know what he'll dream about. It will be the same thing he's dreamed about for the past fifteen years.

III.

THEODORA RUSSELL'S DIARY:
THE ROAD TO SAN FELIPE

Mark Crowden is super white. The chucklehead stands just over six feet tall, weighs approximately 225 pounds, and claims to have golden hair, but I've seen him secretively put lemon juice on it, so I shouldn't have to add that he's vain— *but I will.* He's got a dark-brown goatee with a mustache that's also known as a "vandyke." During an empty moment Mark and I had years ago he volunteered that fact—out of the blue. He's that type. He's in his early forties, though he claims to be thirty-nine, and he has a beer gut that he appears to be proud of—he rubs it unconsciously and enjoys being poked in the stomach by a wayward finger. He willingly tells anyone who will listen that he looks like the artist Ed Kienholz circa 1958. True, he is a doppelganger for Kienholz, but I would alter his self-assessment slightly and say he looks like Kienholz circa

1974, around the time Kienholz put on some unflattering weight.

Poor thing.

When I walked into the Sleepy Eye restaurant he was wearing a serape poncho and an oversized, almost comical, sombrero. He wore them along with some goofy shorts as he sat at a picnic style table eating a bastardized version of a Mexican breakfast: huevos rancheros, French fries, bacon, and fruit. Mr. Dangerous sat next to Mark staring at the food. His large dog eyes nervously alternated between Mark, Joaquin, me, and the food.

Joaquin, who is small and twenty-three, was drinking coffee while Mark ate French fries. He silently attempted to take a fry off Mark's plate but Mark made a growling noise, like a bear, and then swatted Joaquin's hand away with a paper napkin. With his fatso finger Mark pushed a small, pinkish-white watermelon square toward Joaquin. It was whiter than pink and something I would have pitched in the trash if I had been at home. Joaquin put the pathetic watermelon square in his mouth as Mark spoke.

"Of the three of you, Mr. Dangerous is the only one who wasn't bamboozled and didn't give the cop money."

Mark picked up a piece of bacon and put it on the table in front of Mr. Dangerous. Mr. Dangerous sniffed it and then began to contently eat it.

"Fine, *side with the dog*," I said.

I stared at Mark as he picked up a fry and twirled it in the air as if he was urging me to go on at a faster pace, at which point that fat prick put the fry in his mouth and looked down his nose at me as he chewed.

"Ugh! Just frickin' kill me! We were lucky to get out of that situation and it was well worth the forty bucks we spent,"

I said. "Those messed-up Day of the Dead freakazoids could have flipped the SUV! Feel free to hate on me if you want but let me tell you something," I said in a voice that emphasized every word, "those people were desperate enough to do it. They need money and they don't care what they have to do to get it."

Joaquin, good boy that he is, started rambling on about how they wouldn't have flipped the vehicle and how the people of Mexico are nice and how we shouldn't make generalizations, blah, blah, blah. He made a lot of comments based on "goodwill" and giving people the benefit of the doubt. What a fool. All his goodness is annoying. I hate it, hate it, hate it.

Mark hovered over his food and only occasionally glanced up at us with a fake "gritting his teeth" smile. I wanted to slap that smile off his face. He surveyed the table slowly before he locked eyes with Mr. Dangerous. The little bacon eater blinked and looked away as if he didn't like being looked at. I'll say this much for that uppity dog—he was the only one who got any good food out of Mark. When the two of them finished eating, Fatso said, "If we're done we can leave after someone compliments me on my new Latino look."

He stood up, straightened his poncho, and adjusted his sombrero.

Silence.

"Anybody?" asked Mark.

Joaquin moved his head from side to side in a dodgy manner before saying, "That big hat fits your head perfectly."

Gawd! I wanted to splash lye in my eye sockets. As I turned away I said something nonoffensive: "The horizontal stripes in the poncho make me think you went shopping before you had coffee."

More silence.

Mr. Dangerous looked at the three of us and barked. Mark picked him up and kissed him till his tail wagged nonstop. The pooch liked that.

The road to San Felipe is an endless road of emptiness and repetition followed by more of the same. Ten years ago I didn't even know Fric and Frac—now I'm in a foreign country driving down the highway with them. I spent half my life lifting my legs in the air, and this is where it got me.

I met Joaquin through the other one. Like Mark, Joaquin was an orphan. I don't know all the courtroom details, but back in the day Joaquin's entire family was murdered when he was eight. Somewhere in the story there's a family friend who turned out to be a grifter and Joaquin only survived because his mother hid him. It's all sketchy and mysterious and ends with the pony's family being slaughtered. Nobody talks about it because nobody wants to upset Joaquin, which means nobody is a big fat wuss *and* a pussy. Joaquin was a ward of the state from that point forward because he didn't have any extended family that wanted him, which kind of blew. When he used to drink he told me how he spent many a Christmas after he was emancipated. Back then Joaquin lived in a snug courtyard apartment complex, the type with numerous small apartments facing a common landscaped courtyard. His neighbors were gossipy types who inquired about his comings and goings frequently, but he claims it was not in an overly nosy way.

"Oh, you were gone all day Saturday" or "You leave so early in the morning for work."

Sounds like pure pain. I say chatterbox neighbors should mind their own business. I would have smashed a rock through each one of their windows with a threatening note attached. Joaquin, on the other hand, knew one of these neighborhood snoops was always watching, which was reassuring to him and was a deterrent to the roaches that practice crimes like breaking and entering. More than once a neighbor approached Joaquin and informed him of someone who had been to his apartment, knocking on the door or behaving in some other suspicious manner. Two particular neighbors, a set of elderly African American sisters in their nineties would often describe the person in such detail that Joaquin said it bordered on "panoptican," whatever the hell that is.

It was 'cuz of this skanky, skunk scrutiny that on Christmas Day he would put on his best suit of clothes and wrap a large present in the snazziest paper he could find. At the end of his wrapping he would stick a huge, festive bow on the box. Then came the sittin', waitin', and lookin'. He kept his eyes on the windows. When he saw one of his neighbors in the courtyard he would noisily exit his apartment with the big present in hand and wish the neighbor "Merry Christmas" in a loud holiday voice.

Yet orphan boy went to no one's home. Duh. No, that wasn't to be for the sad sack. Instead, he drove to one of the city's nearly vacant parks. He said he preferred Griffith Park or Elysian Park. Once there he would unwrap the present, which wasn't a present at all. It was an empty box. He would throw away the box and keep the paper. Sitting in his truck, he would spend a moment examining the shininess of the paper. Then he would set it aside and either unfold the *Los Angeles Times* or open a book, since he was the reading type. A former smoker, he would have a Christmas cigarette, which would make the little idiot cough and remind him why he quit in the first place, before he went for a long walk within the park.

He said he always encountered a homeless person and engaged them in conversation 'cause it made them both feel "human." Ugh. I hate sappy corn. At the end of their gab fest, which always had to include the merits of sleeping inside as opposed to outside—inside or outside? Outside or inside? Which is preferable?—he would give the homeless person five or ten dollars and wish them a Merry Christmas before continuing his journey.

He would walk down leaf-covered dirt paths in secluded areas and listen to small animals and birds scurry as he approached. Leaves and twigs crunched under his feet. When he was sure no one was around, absolutely sure, he would find a small clearing and kneel down. After making the sign of the cross he would say, out loud, the Lord's Prayer and a Hail Mary. Then he would give special thanks for the home he lived in, his job, and finally for the kindness people had shown him throughout the year. Making the sign of the cross again, he would rise and continue his trek back to his truck in silence. It wasn't a particularly memorable way to spend Christmas, he told me, but it was the only way he knew. When enough time had passed, four hours or so, he would drive back to the courtyard apartments.

All that Christian rap bores my butt big-time, but whenever that nature-loving, prayer-reciting, former smoker annoys me with all that demented Holy Ghost mumbo jumbo, I remember his pathetic "Christmas story" and cut that sad little *niño* some slack.

The first Christmas after they met, Mark selected Joaquin to spend Christmas with. The two hopped into Joaquin's truck, which Mark immediately didn't like (the scrunched-up lemon face was the first clue) because it was too compact and didn't have enough leg room. He kept trying to move the seat back but it wouldn't budge. He glanced over both shoulders over and over again, like that would somehow help. It didn't. Packed in and crowded together they drove to Pasadena searching for a

Christmas meal. Joaquin recounted that it was pouring harder than it had in years and the windshield wipers were one wipe away from being worthless. The only place they could find open was a hamburger joint called Jakes on Colorado Blvd. The few losers in the diner were homeless people nursing soft drinks in an effort to stay out of the rain while the biggest loser of them all, the owner, turned a blind eye to their loitering. Joaquin and Mark sat on stools and ate hamburgers at a counter that looked out onto the rainy street while Christmas music played in the background. Of course, the whole meal was accompanied by the Fat One recounting goofball stories in which he was always the center of attention. It sounds horrible, but Joaquin claims it was his best meal *ever*.

That old, molting peacock Mark Crowden is so full of himself that sometimes I want to throat-punch him. There isn't a bandwagon big enough to house his ego and all his rinky-dink friends. The drunk warbled on once about a swanky pool party he attended back when he wasn't a Big Boy. Upon the putz's entrance into the pool area he slipped on some water and one of his flip-flops went flying, along with Mark. He fell into a small glass table, the glass cracked, Mark's leg was cut, and as he let out a wail everyone rushed to assist him. He was quickly helped to the host's bedroom and put into bed. Once his leg was attended to it was too laborious for him to walk, but this did not ruin the party. Instead the pool party was moved inside and became a slumber party—with Mark at the center holding court from the host's bed. When recounting the story Mark claimed that he really didn't want to be the center of attention, but he's a giant liar. His eyes told me he enjoyed every minute of it.

Mark was given up for adoption when he was a baby, but before he was one year old he was adopted. Mark claims it was because of his good German stock. His birth mother's last name was Bismarck, according to highly secretive papers he found after his father's death, and he's sure, according to those aforementioned documents, that "money exchanged hands."

Mark would pull out photos of himself whenever anyone inquired about his adoption and as he passed the photo to the inquisitor he would yap, yap, yap, "Wasn't I a regal baby? My skin was so white, like the shell of a grade A egg! It's the skin of royalty. I'm probably descended from German nobility."

To stay his friend it was always wise to agree with his cake-hole rambling—on any issue, no matter if it was ultra dorky or Kaiser Wilhelm related. Being an only child, he was treated the way one would expect a childless couple to treat their desperately acquired son.

Yet it shouldn't be surprising that Mark had a smack-down relationship with his mother, a former Miss Long Beach, who unfortunately put on much weight in her later years. Her weight gain and the difficulty it created in her mobility did not deter her from an occasional shopping excursion to Barker Brothers in downtown Los Angeles. Mother Crowden always enjoyed perusing the Barker Brothers' furniture department and seeing her new acquisition in her Manhattan Beach home, which the young Mark kept ass-trembling clean. It was his chore to clean the house and it was his job, as he moved into his teens, to make sure the house ran smoothly. While no one would ever accuse Ma Crowden of anything within the parameters of child abuse, she raised her son in the '60s and '70s and wasn't averse to a little tyranny in the form of hitting him with a belt or slapping him. Mark took exception to this form of parent/child interaction, and to this day he gets peeved if anyone lays a hand on him in an aggressive manner. He'll blurt out whenever anyone playfully slaps him, "I was hit as a child!" He seems to think he was the only one who ever was.

Chuckles didn't just have a difficult relationship with his mother, though. Okay? All his relationships are fraught with difficulty. His friendship with Joaquin only endures because Joaquin is forever willing to swallow his pride and admit some wrong even if he has to search for a way in which he could have been wrong. Joaquin is so clingy and so hell-bent on finding a family that he willingly puts up with him. Mark totally owns Joaquin. Mark's always right and it's not only not unusual but customary for him to completely cut some devastated, bucktoothed, barefooted chump out of his life for some infraction. Once Mark has decided he has been wronged he becomes nonresponsive to all requests for forgiveness. Buh-bye. He is cold and totally hateful with certain people and he has no remorse or guilt. He is able to do this because there are always dopes eager to step up and be Mark's friend. It's a weeding process. He ditches bewildered old friends and individuals who have upset him or he's become tired of and brings in new replacements from the sidelines. This is a continuous, mind-boggling process.

During the year when Mark was sicko, when he was janky-walking like a freak on the lam from a sideshow, Joaquin was always waiting on him hand and foot. Despite the round-the-clock butler and chauffeur service, Mark would get incensed with Joaquin whenever he got into one of his martyr moods.

"Whatever you need me to do is fine with me," that fresh and innocent little plebe would say when Fatso barked out an order.

What Joaquin needed to do was nut up, not take any crap off him, but that's hard for someone like Joaquin. Sure,

I understand the purpose of it all—he had to "visit the sick"—but limits, man. If you're tanked and have no self-respect that's one thing; who hasn't scrawled out life's despairs on a damp cocktail napkin and left it on their crush's doormat? But fumbling and tee-hee-ing over someone, while sober, so they'll *like you*. That's ludicrous behavior.

Joaquin said Mark, who had caller ID, wouldn't pick up the phone one day because he knew it was Joaquin a.k.a. the irritating martyr.

So finally Joaquin left a message and said, "I'm coming over. If you don't open the door when I get there, I'm calling 9-1-1 and the fire department will have to break down your door."

Of course, Mark flung the door open when Joaquin arrived and the little martyr barely had time to frantically pound on the door. Normally I would look down my nose, point a finger, and say the "racing to the rescue" bit was drama for drama's sake, but Joaquin's not that type. He does cares about the well-being of the big white potato.

Mark, who was supporting himself with a cane, was—judging from the wide eyes and overactive, flaring nostrils—about to go ballistic, but Joaquin barely noticed because he was so frickin' happy the sicko wasn't going to have to be carried out feet first. He was giddy with happiness. I suspect it's flattering to have someone, anyone—no matter how codependent—relieved you're alive. So in the end, no matter how wrong it was, giddy happiness trumped seething anger; not only did it trump it, but it turned out to be a crap bulldozer that plowed right through Mark's negative emotions.

Within seconds they were fast friends again. Those two have always had an unspoken, weird bohemian connection between them. They're upset with each other one minute and then suddenly they're not. I don't know how they cross over it so quickly. When I'm in a snit the other person needs to experience fear before I even think of accepting their apology.

But they communicate, time after time, with mere looks or Mark will say a sparse phrase like, "The moan of the modern female is endless," which could refer to me, or "There was a banana exhibit at the snooker parlor today," which I am sure doesn't.

Mark will raise his eyebrows and look at Joaquin over the top of his reading glasses and then Joaquin will get all giggly and start guffawing. I don't know what the hell those two are taking about half the time. They drive me insane with all their secret man talk. This is America, damn it. They need to stop talking like Buzzy Hicks.

Buzzy Hicks was some tool Joaquin lived with in a group home. Joaquin says he never understood what Buzzy was talking about because Buzzy never constructed a story from the beginning. He would throw out random comments and Joaquin had to put the story together later after he reconstructed all the scatterbrain statements into a logical order. Some of that Buzzy Hicks rubbed off onto Joaquin and, via Joaquin, it's certainly jumped and splattered onto Mark.

So on the 9-1-1 evening after Joaquin extorted his way into Mark's digs, Mark ended up making dinner for him. Wrong. Of course that wasn't how it happened. What happened was Mark sat at the kitchen table, switching his cane from one hand to the other while reading the newspaper. When he had finished one story but hadn't started the next he directed Joaquin on what to do; what ingredients to add, how much, and when. The dish ended up being shepherd's pie, which, by the way, is Mark's favorite.

My head jerked toward the front seat when I heard Mark yell, "Stop!" Mark was excitedly and frantically asking where the toilet paper and sani-wipes were and Joaquin was pulling off onto the shoulder of the road. They both scrambled out of the vehicle and Joaquin opened the back of the SUV for Mark, who quickly started throwing things about and then grabbing what he needed before scampering off into the rugged terrain. There were large boulders scattered throughout the landscape with mountains in the distance. Mark ran about a hundred feet and then made a quick left behind a huge boulder. Then we couldn't see him anymore. Probs?

Joaquin stood looking off into the distance and said, "It must have been the huevos rancheros."

I got out to stretch and Joaquin let Mr. Dangerous out, too, so he could do his dirty little dog business. We were the only car in the landscape. Mr. Dangerous was sniffing the ground and found a small salamander, which that wacko dog tried to eat. Joaquin got overly excited and freaked like he was having a bad trip. He picked up Mr. Dangerous and tried to get the salamander out of Mr. D's mouth. The salamander's tail, which stuck out between Mr. Dangerous's lips, was the only sign of what he had consumed. Joaquin was trying to insert his finger into Mr. Dangerous's mouth from the side, but he wasn't too successful, so I asked what the big deal was. It was a tiny salamander. Right?

"Let him eat it."

Joaquin looked at me with an unfathomable look upon his face, as if I was completely void of any pet knowledge. He had an edge to his voice when he spoke.

"If he eats it he'll throw up all the way to San Felipe. Do you want a sick dog hacking up salamander bits sitting beside you in the car?"

When Joaquin began performing the Heimlich maneuver on the salamander's foe I decided to have a cigarette and let the two of them wrestle it out. Mr. D. finally spat out the salamander, which flew about five feet before landing near my feet. The saliva-covered reptile looked gross and confused before it regained its bearings and made a lightning-fast getaway. Mr. Dangerous was wiggling and trying to get out of Joaquin's arms, so Joaquin set him down, but even though he sniffed and tried to find the salamander again, he couldn't.

Mr. D. turned his pent-up dog energy back at Joaquin and attacked his white sock with gusto. The Fat One says whenever D-Dog is attacking a sock he's thinking one of three things. It's either "Dagnabit!" "Doggone it!" or "Curse you!" I puffed on my cigarette and watched. His head moved back and forth vigorously as he pulled at the sock and growled.

Personally, I opt for the third one, but with a different verb.

It was during this sock attack that Mark came running back to the SUV. He looked disoriented and his goofy shorts were around his ankles. Fortunately, the serape poncho was long enough to hide the one thing Mark shows only on a need-to-know basis.

Out of breath he said, "I think I saw the Chupacabras."

I said, "What?"

Joaquin said, "What?"

Mr. Dangerous looked at Mark and made a sound that sounded like "what?"

Mark looked at Mr. Dangerous with a quizzical look and repeated, "I think I saw the Chupacabras."

He hurriedly spoke. "I found this medium-size rock behind that big boulder there." He pointed to the boulder we had seen him run behind earlier. "Anyway, I sat on this medium-size rock with my butt sticking over the edge because I had to go number two."

Those four dead presidents in Rapid City express more emotion on their stone faces than Joaquin and I expressed at that moment. Joaquin held two fingers up to his lips and looked at me with sketchy eyes—like a Mexican Mona Lisa. He tapped his lips with his fingers before he bent down and picked up Mr. Dangerous.

Mark continued. "So I'm sitting there and I hear this chittering noise. It was kind of like the sound a squirrel makes but not as squirrelly, *yet evil sounding.*"

Neither Joaquin nor I responded. Mr. Dangerous turned his head to the side. His tongue stuck out between his lips.

"So I'm looking around and I see some movement over by this big, dried-out bush. I see the bush start to shake a little and then this blur runs from behind the bush to behind a large rock nearby. Well, right then and there I decided I was getting the H out of there, and as I stood up this large weird coyote-type animal took off running from behind the rock, but it was too fat to be a coyote. It kind of looked like a wolf with *huge* fangs."

I blew some smoke in Mark's direction and watched as it encircled his head. I raised my eyebrows noticeably before I turned away from him.

"What," he asked as he threw his hands up in the air with a perturbed look upon his face.

I turned back, and after taking a long drag off my cigarette said, "You're a crazypants."

Mark stared at me without blinking. Then he stared at me some more without blinking. Joaquin said later that it was almost "cyclopean" in its intensity.

Joaquin asked, "Did you bring back my sani-wipes?"

Mark stared at Joaquin just as unblinkingly as he did with me. He didn't respond. He looked at us both for a few more seconds before he very deliberately bent over and pulled up his shorts. He walked over to the SUV's passenger door, opened it, and got in. The door slammed shut. Joaquin and I looked at Mark sulking in the vehicle. He really is a big juvenile.

Joaquin made a succinct comment when he uttered faintly, "Uh-oh."

Joaquin, Mr. Dangerous, and I climbed back into the SUV.

While there was complete silence from Mr. D. and me, Joaquin, who was in the driver's seat, turned to Mark solemnly and looked at him momentarily before he spoke. I was hoping he wouldn't bone it and was relieved that he saved us all a lot of agony and groaning when he said, "I'm sorry I did not take your Chupacabras sighting seriously. That was wrong of me. If it ever happens again, I will."

Mark grunted and it was obvious he wanted to speak but he had a bug up his butt that stopped him.

"Forgive me?"

Mark grunted again, but he really had no other option. What was he going to do? Not talk to either one of us the entire time we were in Mexico? My people reading skills told me Fatty McCrowden finally recognized the advantage of *not* bullying and bitching at everybody.

Mark said, "Play my song and I'll feel better."

Mark handed Joaquin an old CD and Joaquin put it in the CD player. After Mark quickly pushed some buttons, out of the stereo speakers came Steely Dan's "Rikki Don't Lose That Number." This sappy concoction of loss and desperation is

Mark's *most* favorite song, and everyone he meets eventually discovers this piece of Fatboy musical trivia. He actually tells people that he wants them to remember him when they hear that song. I originally found it totally bonkers that someone would ask me to remember them, but in retrospect shouldn't that be rule number one for all the sad, attention-addicted people in the world? Years ago, between cigarette puffs, Joaquin brought up a highfalutin theory by a snooty French theorist who asserted the act of viewing old photographs was the return of the dead; that when old photographs are viewed, the sitter's life, existence, and mortality are acknowledged. Mark, according to Joaquin, was asking the same thing of his friends, not through photographs but rather through music.

Whatever.

It was his song and no one else could claim it. So, as Mark sat in the front seat singing, Mr. Dangerous climbed his way into the front seat and stood on Mark's lap. He licked Mark on the neck and ears as he sang. Geez, I'm gonna need an oversized hankie to spit all my upchuck into.

Four minutes later.

Unfortunately, after the song was over Joaquin tried to start the car but it was dead.

Since neither of these knuckleheads even changes his own oil, we unloaded our luggage, including Mr. D's cage, and set it all next to the SUV. Mark decreed we would "hitch" a ride the rest of the way.

While we waited, Mark pretended he was Frankenstein. With the oversized sombrero on his head and clothed in the serape poncho, he walked with stiff outstretched arms and stiff legs. Mr. Dangerous barked and jumped around at Mark's feet. I sat on my luggage and had a cigarette while Joaquin raced around like some pushy paparazzi taking pictures of us all. He said he was going to put them in a scrapbook and call it "Our Adventure in Mexico."

Approximately half an hour later—it takes me seven minutes to smoke a ciggy and I was on my fifth one—a large panel truck drove up slowly. It looked like it would be used to transport small animals or construction supplies. The cab of the truck was rusted and banged up, and it was from the late 1950s or early 1960s. When the vehicle stopped Joaquin talked to the driver and explained we needed a ride to San Felipe with *all* our luggage. The driver, who had big nostrils, said he would give us a ride for twenty dollars—American. Joaquin agreed but would only give him the money when we got to San Felipe. He also mentioned we wanted to be taken to a place where we could get some transportation. The driver nodded and got out of the truck to let us ride in the back. We followed him and watched as he took a large wooden gate off the back of the truck and the five of us, including Mr. D., stood there looking at the driver's cargo. They were large Latina women with big arms and big legs, women with big torsos, thick necks, and big hair. Outfit-wise they were all decked out in lingerie; they wore garter belts and stockings and high heels and bustiers and short slips. They looked like farm girls who had found a profession that would keep them away from all types of animals except big, fat *cochinos*.

The ladies in lingerie smiled and said, *"Vente, vente."*

They nodded and urged us to come forward with their eyes and hands. Mr. Dangerous was scared. He blinked his eyes and looked around. Mark told Joaquin to get in the truck and he started handing the luggage up to him. I climbed in and Mr. D. sat on my lap with his ears back. He usually doesn't like to sit on my lap, but he did this time. He kept looking up at me for reassurance. Once the luggage was loaded, Mark jumped in and the driver slipped the gate back into place. I could hear the driver walk to the cab's door, get in, and start up the truck. It was a breezy ride with the four of us staring at the four women. Joaquin asked if they were going to a costume party, but they all giggled at his question like teenage girls who had a secret. They told Joaquin they were "entertainers."

"Entertainers," Mark exclaimed. "Show us what you do."

Joaquin translated and the ladies giggled again. The largest one, who was painted up very garishly but not much differently than a super-trashy runway slut, rose on her large, square platform heels. She clasped her hands together and followed them up with the grace of a belly dancer. On her feet, she moved her body by following her hands. With her arms extended in front of her and slightly bent she showed her audience her palms and moved them and her body in a continuous left and right direction like a hula dancer. Yet as an "entertainer" she added her own special seduction technique, which entailed suddenly stopping the graceful arm and body movements to shake her heinie rather vulgarly. In all deference to her, there really is no graceful way to shake your heinie in a fifty-year-old truck speeding down a highway in Mexico. While she danced Mark winked at her and blew kisses, which just egged her on, but I noticed Fatboy kept his wallet in his back pocket. Her skanky dance came to an abrupt end when the truck hit a bump and she threw herself into Mark's arms. They both laughed and then Mark closed his eyes and cocked his head to the side so his cheek could be kissed. She looked at Mark in a confused manner before she kissed his cheek…rather hesitantly. I suspect she is the one who is normally kissed. One of the other ladies pulled out a guitar while another picked up her green tambourine. The four of them sang Mexican folk songs that, according to Joaquin, were about the plight of women and the men that cause their plights.

I hear you, *señorita*.

When we finally arrived at San Felipe we unloaded our luggage and Mark and Joaquin helped the "entertainers" down to stretch and bid us good-bye. It was then, as we all stood at the back of the truck, that the one who'd *danced* asked where we were going exactly. Joaquin's response caused them to react in a way that I did not anticipate: all four, in unison, gasped. They all started blabbing at once in hurried panicked tones. According to Joaquin they urged us not to go and said we should turn around and go back to America—"the land of gold and riches." They begged us to reconsider our decision. They crossed themselves and one began reciting prayers in Spanish. The dancer took a cross on a chain out of her bra and put it in Mark's hand. She removed his sombrero and placed the cross around his neck. Then the other three scavenged their lingerie. The one who played the guitar took a cross out of her garter and put it around Joaquin's neck. The one with the tambourine took a cross out of her shoe and gave it to me, and the fourth one spent a good deal of time searching in her panties for a cross. She seemed to have lost it. When she finally found it she put it around Mr. Dangerous's neck. Their faces gave me the chills but piqued my interest.

What was this about? Mark and Joaquin thanked them and Mark stuck out his cheek and allowed each of them to kiss him. As we turned and walked away we could hear them praying on our behalf in Spanish. Ahead of me I could hear Joaquin softly say in English what they said in Spanish,

"And forgive us our trespasses as we forgive those who trespass against us, and lead us not into temptation, but deliver us from evil. Amen."

IV.
JOAQUIN MORENO'S JOURNAL: THE THREE LINKS

Mark and Theodora stood next to each other and stared at me.

"I'm not riding a donkey," Theodora said. "I'm a lady!" She pointed at herself in a twitchy manner when she uttered the word *lady* and then pulled out a half-smoked cigarette from her purse, lit it, and glared.

Mark tilted his head down at an angle and looked at her out of the corner of his eye. He turned his head slightly away from her when he said, "Joaquin will pay for the donkey rental."

Theodora pointed her finger at Mark and bristled as she said, "Don't start with me."

My problem was I hadn't been specific enough with the driver. I assumed he knew that I meant *car* transportation. I didn't think to say, "We *don't* want donkey transportation."

Mark kept saying, "I want to ride the donkey. I want to ride the donkey. I want to ride the donkey."

Every time he said it, Theodora gave him the finger.

I looked at Theodora and said, "That's not very ladylike."

Theodora's cranky response was to give me the finger too.

"Look," I explained, "the tow company won't be able to retrieve the car till tomorrow. It's only three miles to the house. If we take the donkeys we'll make it there in an hour or two. Plus, they have cool little carts that they pull."

"We can form a donkey caravan," Mark exclaimed.

Theodora stared at Mark for a moment and then threw her lit cigarette at his chest. It bounced off his stomach and fell to the ground.

Mark looked down at the cigarette and said to me in a whisper, "Isn't she going to need that later?"

Theodora finally agreed to go via donkey if, as Mark put it, she could "pimp her ride." From that I assumed she was going to find a big metal chain with an enormous clock attached to it and put it around her donkey's neck but, no, instead she just bought a standard wreath of flowers for her burro's neck and a big, green, floppy straw hat for his head. We took pictures of everyone on their donkey and I took a great picture of Mr. Dangerous cheek to cheek with Mark's donkey. Judging from the wary look on Mr. D.'s face, he either didn't like the donkey or he thought the donkey stank.

Mark led our donkey caravan. Theodora had the second spot, and I brought up the rear. Each of us had our luggage stacked in our own donkey cart. I put Mr. D's cage in my cart but Mr. D. in Theodora's cart so I could watch him. The donkeys moved rather slowly, but that enabled us to the see the city at a leisurely pace.

There was a great deal of traffic downtown. It was chaotic and noisy due to all the vehicles with loud mufflers and the constant honking of horns. As we passed by some neon signs advertising Mexican beers I noticed an Indian couple with dark skin and angular, indigenous features on the sidewalk. They stood motionless in their native dress. They appeared to be modern-day tobacco statues. Farther down the street there was an old cinema from the 1960s with its original marquee right next to a little café with a sign that said *"Nunca nos cerramos."* A man in a white apron swept the sidewalk in front of the café. True, it was picturesque but as I looked to the curb, where he swept his refuse, I noticed a big rat crawling into the gutter.

While we did hear the rhythm of a gentle bossanova, it came from a tavern with two borrachos slugging it out on the sidewalk near the front door. Mr. D. saw a cute Chihuahua on the sidewalk and it was obvious from his pacing, panting, and whining that he wanted to get out of the cart and *go say "hi,"* but the Chihuahua ignored Mr. D. and kept her nose in the air as she passed by. Mr. D. looked at me with sad eyes as she trotted off.

"She probably has a boyfriend," I said.

His ears perked up as he listened to me and he barked.

The lights didn't always illuminate the nicer aspects of San Felipe. Along the way we passed a structure that appeared to be a house of ill repute. Ladies dressed very similarly to those in our hitched ride stood in front of the establishment and waved at the passing traffic. We waved back, which only made them hoot and purr at us in suggestive ways. I'm sure the locals thought we were crazy gringos, riding the donkeys and all, but we didn't care. When we reached the city limits we stopped. We pulled up beside each other and looked at the barren landscape before us. I stared at the dry, sandy emptiness of it all.

Mark took off his sombrero and wiped his forehead with the inside of his forearm before he replaced his hat. After scanning the landscape silently, he smiled as he turned and looked from Theodora to me. He clicked his tongue, moved his donkey forward and yelled, *"Mule traiiiinnnnn!"*

Theodora, with a cigarette dangling from her lips, said, "Giddyup," and followed Mark.

As I watched the two of them move away, Mr. Dangerous stared at me from the back of Theodora's cart. He moved his head from side to side and barked.

I got in line.

We discovered, as we plodded along, that the donkeys moved no faster on a country dirt road than on a downtown city street, and possibly even slower. I had folded a blanket very carefully, to maximize its plushness, for Mr. Dangerous to sleep on, and he looked quite content as he snoozed away in Theodora's cart. Theodora had taken the big hat off her donkey and was wearing it herself. In the hot sun it was a smart move. I remember what Mark said about her right before he introduced me years ago.

"She's no lady," he claimed. "She's somewhere on that fine line between a tramp and a modern woman, and the day determines which one she is."

I'll admit she looked like she smoked too much, but there were still traces of her youth and beauty under all the smoke damage. She had been working for a carnival as a burlesque dancer when Mark first met her in a bar called the Strongman;

it had a moving neon sign above the door depicting a man in a leotard who lifted a barbell from his chest to above his head in a jerky neon movement. The Strongman was one of those trendy bars that brought back old-timey acts as new. They wanted vintage acts with a new twist. Plate spinners, ventriloquists, comedy duos, sister acts (usually singers), xylophone players, and burlesque dancers were just some of the acts the Strongman booked.

Theodora had been auditioning to do a weekly show for the owner of the Strongman, and while she hadn't moved into leathery, old sailor territory she wasn't twenty anymore, but thirty-eight. Mark suspected Theodora was on the verge of being subjected to the grimy underside of showbiz and she must have suspected it, too, because she didn't hesitate when Mark offered her a job in his Pasadena architectural firm that same evening. He hardly knew her and it was rather impetuous and irrational for him to hire her on the spot, but when he discovered she was an Aries, like himself, they immediately became fast friends. The liquor Mark consumed probably had something to do with the job offer, too. He has always tended to drink to excess. There is something that drives him to drink, and that combined with his desire to be a "man about town" has led to many of the tangled problems he has had to deal with throughout his life.

Hiring Theodora was not a mistake per se. She was quite efficient and learned quickly. She was his receptionist and assistant in a firm that had seven architects. According to Mark she dressed rather "showy" and often appeared at work looking like she had just stepped out of a 1940s film or "off a street corner," but that wasn't necessarily the reason why the other women in the office disliked her or judged her. To be more precise, it was the fact that she was exceedingly honest about her past, and the male sex tends to talk about a woman's past even more than the female sex. Once a male employee or a male client found out that Theodora was a former burlesque dancer, they wanted to meet her and learn more about it, "it" being the burlesque dancing. While I wouldn't say Theodora lacked the qualities of decency and propriety, I have come to the conclusion that different people have different standards. Mark claims there were times when he would come out of his office to find Theodora performing an old routine in front of her desk for a male client. While she wouldn't be wearing pasties and a G-string, it was still inappropriate for the workplace. Mark would smile till the end of the performance, deal with the male client, and then admonish Theodora privately and request she not perform her old routines at work.

"You're not working the midway anymore," Mark would say, exasperated. "This is Pasadena!"

Theodora would be very apologetic and promise to refrain from any more impromptu office performances, but heaven help her, there was just something in her being that made her want to strut around in front of men and lift up her legs.

Fortunately, Mark was more architectural historian during this period than architect. After fifteen years, he had grown weary of being an architect, trying to accommodate the needs of clients when what the clients wanted wasn't what Mark was interested in designing. Sure, he still worshiped those in the pantheon of architecture: FLW, Adler & Sullivan, H.H. Richardson, Burnham and Root, Alvar Aalto, Le Corbusier, Cass Gilbert, and their ilk, but he wasn't interested in dealing with clients and *their* uninspired taste.

He marveled, like everyone else, upon the completion of Frank Gehry's Disney Concert Hall. Days before the building officially opened there was a public open house; we went, and outside of Mark having to urinate and not being able to find an unlocked men's room until the very end of the tour, he enjoyed it immensely. He simply seems more interested in rediscovering old buildings now, and uncovering the context in which they were designed and built. This is part of the impetus for our journey to San Felipe. From the photographs we've seen, the Victorian house we're on the verge of purchasing has not only, in Mark's words, "an Eastlake exterior but also a pre-Raphaelite interior."

Theodora has claimed Mark is snotty, but I suspect she misspoke and the word she really meant to use was "snobby." Her disparaging comment, in this instance, was the result of a conversation I had with Mark—which I related to her—concerning the destruction of architecturally significant buildings.

I said to him in passing, "It's a crime that gold-and-white monument to the sewing machine, the Singer Building, was destroyed. Whenever I see images of the current NYC skyline I still search for it even though it's been forgotten by practically every single person on the planet."

Turning to him, I asked which building he wished had avoided the wrecker's ball. He pondered my question as if it was of great importance, but in spite of that he responded unexpectedly. He didn't propose to rescue an American skyscraper from the early twentieth century or one of those opulent movie palaces from the 1920s. Instead he picked a foreign building, the Barcelona Pavilion. When I recounted the story to her, Theodora responded to the words *the Barcelona Pavilion* with a sickened look. Not that she knew what it was.

The Barcelona Pavilion was a temporary building built in 1928, I explained. "It stood for less than a year."

Theodora stared intensely at me as I continued.

"It was a small structure constructed of marble and glass that was situated next to a shallow pool. There was a statue and a few chairs within the building, but the prevailing element was empty space—lots of empty space with no adornment."

Theodora waited for me to say more but when she realized I had finished, she said, "Well, that's just stupid. Why would he pick *that* building?"

I searched for a reason. "It was elegant, I guess."

Theodora first made a face that had repugnance swirled all about it then she said, "Oh, he's so hoity-toity and *snotty*. It's because it was French and foreign—that's why he picked it. You know him. That is so him."

I did know him and I knew her, too, so I didn't think it was the right moment to mention that Barcelona was in Spain. Instead I sat there and looked at her as I said, "Snotty?"

Theodora crossed her arms over her chest and nodded nonstop as I repeated the word over and over again.

"Snotty? *Snotty?* SNOTTY?"

Theodora impatiently tapped her foot, which led me to believe she wasn't finished with our conversation. I'm not averse to gossiping, but I didn't want to end up with a nasty taste in my mouth, so I proceeded with caution.

"Did I tell you what he said after his car accident?"

Theodora stopped nodding and started shaking her head, but she did it very slowly and squinted her eyes as if she wasn't going to believe what came out of my mouth.

"He was driving that black Honda at the time."

Theodora didn't respond, but I knew she knew which car I meant.

"It was the one with the crashed-in passenger side. It was so caved in the glove compartment wouldn't open and the window wouldn't roll up."

"So what did he say?" Theodora blurted out impatiently. "Everybody knows he ran that car straight into the ground."

I heard her demand, but I still wanted to get in one last comment: "I wouldn't ride in it because I always had to ride in the back since I *couldn't* sit in the front. For me, it was too Miss Daisy-ish."

Theodora nodded in agreement, as if there were some thresholds that could not be crossed and sitting in the backseat, for an adult, was one of them.

"So finally the Honda sputtered its way to its grave, which in this instance was that big slab of concrete that sat behind his duplex."

I referred to the concrete slab that was only accessible via a narrow back alleyway. There were some dead plants in cracked plastic pots sitting on the slab, an old river rock birdbath more frequented by squirrels than birds, and a barbecue grill Mark no longer used. Rusting away on the slab, the old black Honda became a home for the neighborhood's feral cats. I would sometimes peer into it and there would be masses of cat fur nestled in the seats, and occasionally a startled cat awakened from its slumber looked up at me with both surprise and fear. During this time, while he tried to decide which new car to purchase, Mark still had to get around.

I became his chauffeur; he frequently called me for rides and often, on the weekends, I put off my own errands so we could do his. He rarely thanked me but it didn't upset me. Really.

"So, he's always asking me for rides," I said to Theodora.

"Sounds like him."

"But I couldn't be there all the time."

"Uh-huh," said Theodora as she nodded.

"So I told him maybe he should get one of those little grocery carts so when he goes to the store he wouldn't have to carry all his groceries home."

Theodora did an eye roll. In a deadpan voice she said, "What did that ass clown say?"

"He said no to my suggestion because *he had a reputation in the neighborhood.*"

Theodora threw her head back and snorted with laughter. "Reputation?" she said. "He's got a reputation, all right."

I did begin to giggle as Theodora laughed and flailed her arms around her head in a manic, crazy, chasing-away-a-gnat manner.

She was all keyed up with laughter as she said, "He's got a reputation as the guy who stumbles home drunk from the bar—while eating a big burrito—with the sauce spilling all over the front of his shirt! *That's* his reputation."

"That's Mark," I said. "He even did it when he had that gammy leg. Remember?"

Theodora nodded as she continued to laugh. "Oh, I remember the gammy leg."

Yet architecture would rank fourth in Mark's lineup of what is important. First, of course, would be his huge spirit and everything that entails, including his reputation.

Second would be eating. This accounts for Mark's robust size. He's certainly overweight, not fat—yet, but that appears to be where he is headed.

Third would be reading; when at home Mark is practically always holding a book. It's like he has an extra appendage. He likes murder mysteries by female authors, especially Agatha Christie, followed by modern fiction by women authors in general. He can usually be found in his rumpled bed engrossed in some new book. It is not uncommon for him to read late into the night, to go to sleep only after he has finished reading the last sentence in the last chapter and to suffer the consequences of his actions the following morning when the alarm clock rings. The one thing that can pull him away from a book is food. There is usually some foodstuff around him, either on the nightstand or on a bed tray. Once, while staying at his home while mine was being rewired, I gently knocked on his bedroom door and entered to discover him, in bed, with a book in one hand and a pork chop in the other. It was one of those razor-thin pork chops and he had his teeth on the edge of it. His eyes diverted from his book to me. He didn't say anything but his eyes asked, "Did you want something?" I looked at him, remained mute, and took a step back. As I began to close the door, his attention returned to his book and I could see his front teeth nibbling on the pork chop like a hungry zoo animal. As the door clicked closed I could hear him humming *and* chewing.

He's always had a hearty resilience. After his surgery and convalescence, when he finally regained his movement, I remember on that first New Year's Eve he wanted to stay home. It was his habit. He found the atmosphere of bars too depressing to bring in the New Year. It was a strange stance for someone so gregarious, for someone who lived off the attention of others and whose affability blossomed even more because of that attention. He claimed on New Year's Eve everyone is trying *so hard* to have a "huffle and kerfuffle"—which is his code for something else—that the whole atmosphere reeks of hungry desperation, and of course, Markie finds hungry desperation extremely disgusting.

"It's repulsive," he claimed. "The night is filled with

nonsense, vanity, and worst of all, the wrong sort of people. I wouldn't think of being seen out on New Year's Eve. There's too much unbridled pandemonium."

Whenever he would say this, and he said it every year, he would squeeze his eyes closed and shake his head and shoulders wincingly when he got to the word *pandemonium*, as if it was all so beneath him.

On that particular New Year's Eve while I looked through his old CDs, which included way too many disco hits for my taste, he turned on the radio. I looked up when I heard the knob's click and I had no idea what he was up to, but there in the middle of the dining room beside the oak table he inherited from a lost, dead friend, he began to dance. He did a version of that old Chubby Checker hit, the Twist, yet he did it with a little extra energy that made it border on the frantic; it was a lead-footed Twist but he made up for it with super-fast, diesel-charged hip and arm movement.

"Look at me," he said with a big grin on his face.

I stared at him, unsure how to react.

"I can dance again."

The look on his face became clear. The monumental smile was so filled with accomplishment that it overtook his face and radiated forth what was in his head; his eyes begged me to agree with him.

"I'm back to the way I was," he proclaimed breathlessly.

All I knew was he was quite proud of himself. I sat down and nodded as he proved to me he was the man he was before.

While Mark's disposition was generally sunny, to the casual observer Theodora seemed to have a hostile streak within her that occasionally rose up toward the most innocuous individuals and groups. She constantly complained about interactions she had with both the handicapped and seniors, claiming both groups were "pushy" and "demanding." Theodora wanted to know why the elderly person with a cane who could barely walk and moved slowly always wanted to stand in the front and be the first to disembark public transportation, leaving the able-bodied passengers who were still agile to wait behind.

The week before our departure she said the following in conversation: "They think they're so frickin' special and everybody is supposed to kowtow to them just because they're old. I say wait in the back, old biddy. Let me out first and then you can shuffle your way over to the pharmacy or the old folks' home or the cemetery."

Sigh.

Even her goal, which she's sporadically mentioned, has a sour bite. In the past, she's talked about opening a bookstore and café. The bookstore would be in the rear with the café up front. The café would be open to everyone while the bookstore would be restricted. She's indignant about that and won't change her mind. Access to the bookstore would be via membership and offered only to women. No men allowed! I don't know if it's possible to operate a business successfully that excludes 50 percent of the American population, but she plans on charging exorbitant prices to compensate. She's said she would give the food and drink "special" names to move them: a lady latte, a female Frappuccino, a gal gelato. I won't repeat her special name for the tea, but it's going to be the most expensive and it was designed to titillate men.

Don't misunderstand, Theodora likes men, but she finds them immensely insufferable much of the time and wants a retreat from their "finkdom." She plans on calling the place the Sisterhood Bookshop. I suspect she would let me in if I asked, but there's no way she would allow Mark entrance. She once whispered in my ear that his picture would be posted at the female security guard's desk with a missing tooth and a blackened eye. Of course, Theodora would scratch the disfigurements in herself with the aid of an angry ballpoint pen. A note under his photo would say something along the line of *No chumps allowed and specifically this chump.*

I determined it was best not to mention anything about it to Mark because if he knew he would crinkle up his nose and get peeved—mainly that someone would deface his photo.

It is not always clear to me how Theodora became my friend. She sometimes utters statements that seem to run against everything I have tried to do in my service to my fellow man. One of the first things I'm going to do upon our arrival is explain to her the tenets of our "Secret Society."

Our destination, Cascada, was in sight, and it was as grand as I expected. This huge Victorian Eastlake house stood on a cliff overlooking the Gulf of California. It must have been built circa 1880 but by whom I didn't know. The grounds surrounding the home were lush and green with a scattering of tropical vegetation and trees. There was a stairway leading from the edge of the cliff down to the beach below, made of concrete with a simple metal railing. After we hitched our donkeys to some trees, I released Mr. D. to sniff the grass. It was then, as we approached the house, that we noticed two men standing on the porch. One of them stayed on the porch while the other approached us. He was tall, about six feet. He had thinning hair and a very bushy salt-and-pepper mustache. He was dressed in dungarees and a button-down shirt and instantly caused jealousy in me, and I'm sure Mark, because he was in great athletic shape. He met us halfway and extended his hand. Despite saying "welcome," his face carried a look of concern.

He introduced himself with, *"Yo soy Señor De La Santos."*

We exchanged pleasantries and he pointed to the donkeys.

"I did not expect you to arrive by burro."

Mark explained what had happened with our SUV and Mr. De La Santos listened with intensity to every word. After hearing the recounted events, he said he would drive into town later and see if he could get the vehicle working and back to us by dusk.

As we approached the house, the man who had remained on the porch descended the steps. He was a short, chubby man who was approximately fifty years old with thick white hair. He wore reading glasses propped on the edge of his nose even though he wasn't reading and was dressed, in Mark's words, "rather meticulously." Not only was he wearing wingtips, dress slacks, and a dress shirt, but he had on a vest and tie—in this heat.

He extended his hand and addressed Theodora and Mark when he said, "You must be the master and mistress?"

While no one corrected him, introductions ensued, and we discovered him to be Lord Leighton, who, as Mr. De La Santos put it, "would like to be your first guest." We talked on the porch as Mr. De La Santos wrangled with the front door's lock. He turned it left and then right and then left again. He turned it all around clockwise and then all around counterclockwise and I watched and hoped he wasn't making it worse. There was a quirky element involved in unlocking the door and I concluded there must be some trick.

Mark walked up to Mr. De La Santos and said, "Let me try."

He bent slightly and turned the key to the right, to three

o'clock, there was a click, and with one large hand on each door Mark cautiously pushed the double doors open. We all turned and looked.

It was huge.

We walked into an entry hall that engulfed us. Three stories high and probably thirty feet square, it had a circular wooden staircase that wrapped around the room from the first floor to the third floor.

Theodora summed up all of our feelings when she said, "Holy Toledo!" Her voice echoed around the room just as our footsteps did on the waxed floor.

There was one extraordinary room after another; many of the rooms appeared to be papered in William Morris wallpapers, not the reproduction kind but rather the original papers from the end of the nineteenth century. Aesthetic furniture was everywhere and while I could be mistaken, I'm positive there were authentic, undocumented paintings by Dante Gabriel Rossetti, Edward Burne-Jones, John Everett Millais, and Holman Hunt adorning the walls. Theodora's assessment of Cascada was that it was "kicky." Lord Leighton said it's "from ever so long ago and perfectly preserved." As an architectural historian Mark was thrilled and saddened: thrilled because interiors along this line rarely exist anymore, saddened because there was nothing for him to reconstruct and nothing for him to fix.

As he stood and scanned one of the rooms he said in an almost inaudible voice, "I can document these interiors. Someone should, at least, do that."

We all selected bedrooms on the second floor adjacent to one another. I selected the one with a wall of cobalt blue tile going three-quarters of the way up the wall and framing two stained-glass windows. The woodwork surrounding the windows was painted white and the images depicted in the windows were of Maximilian and Carlota. The other three walls were papered in the William Morris trellis pattern. With a sky-colored background, it had a trellis pattern of ivy, small flowers, and birds intertwined throughout it. There was a bedstead of Mission design in fumed oak with a matching dresser.

After unpacking my clothes and neatly placing them in the dresser, I stood on a chair, and on the wall closest to the door, attaching it to the picture rail with two dress slack hangers—the kind that clamp onto the trousers' cuffs—I hung my "Secret Society" curtain, a wall hanging, really—the one Mark referred to as moth-eaten. It's not moth-eaten. Well, maybe there are two or three moth holes, but overall they're almost undetectable within the design. I paid $600 for it, but it was worth double that price. Made of wool and still smelling like wool one hundred years after it was woven, it is two feet wide by six feet high with red symbols upon a pale mustard-colored background.

The symbols include the beehive, scythe, dove, cross, three links, hourglass, bundle of rods, casket, skull and crossbones, All-Seeing Eye, world, arrows, three pillars, "hand with heart," scales, serpent, hatchet, alter of incense, Ark of the Covenant, open Bible, and the Ten Commandments.

Downstairs, in the main parlor on the first floor, under a large gilded cast-iron chandelier is a Mason & Hamlin grand piano made of mahogany. Mark, who spent many a Saturday afternoon in his youth practicing the piano under his mother's direction, was playing. His musical education began on one of those dark brown, hard plastic, tabletop Allen organs that seemed to be prevalent in the 1960s, but when his mother discovered he had an affinity for music she switched him to the piano. The sound found its way up to my bedroom. I knew it was Mark because the song was "Clair de Lune." Mark always starts his recitals with "Clair de Lune." This would be followed by "Moon River" from *Breakfast at Tiffany's*. These were not Mark's favorite songs necessarily, though he had become fond of them over the years; rather they were his mother's favorite songs, and since she was his instructor, these were the songs he knew best.

I walked into the hallway and knocked on Theodora's door. Theodora opened it only a crack. I could see part of her face and a haze of smoke encircling her head.

"I want to tell you a secret but you can't tell anybody— ever," I said.

Theodora looked at me quizzically.

"When you finish your cigarette come across the hall."

Theodora didn't say anything, and with her customary tact shut the door in my face.

I walked back across the hall and left my door open for her. She's really slovenly sometimes. I suspect it's due to the toxicity of her cigarettes; the more she smokes, the more lethargic she becomes. As I waited, I looked out the window at a towering structure sitting on a hill less than a mile away. I deduced I must be seeing the rear of the building because it appeared to be merely an impregnable wall with vertical slits and no other surface decoration. I'll have to ask Mr. De La Santos about it.

A few minutes later Theodora walked into my room and sat down in an oversized rocking chair that sat near the end of the bed. She appeared fatigued and I marked it down to the long donkey ride.

"You paying attention?" I asked.

Theodora didn't respond. She just stared at me.

"Okay, this is the secret part. Mark and I belong to a secret society." I paused and looked to see if there was any reaction in her eyes. I wasn't sure, so I continued. "This secret society originated in 1819 and it's called the Odd Fellowship. Mark and I are both Odd Fellows."

I'll say this much for her, she didn't smile *or* laugh. She sat stone-faced. I continued, "The mission of the Odd Fellows is to visit the sick, relieve the distressed, bury the dead, and educate orphans. We try to live by a certain code. We try to live in a positive manner. We try to be better people." I paused. "It's about goodness and love. Does any of this make any sense?"

Theodora looked at me suspiciously and asked, "What are you saying, exactly?"

I thought for a second and then looked at the curtain. "Let's try it this way." I walked over to my suitcase and pulled out an old leather book with a repaired spine and a gilt image depicting an Odd Fellow upon its cover. It was the Odd-Fellow Manual from 1852 by Aaron Grosh. I continued, "This is the Odd-Fellow Manual." I held the book out and shook it a little in front of Theodora. I pointed to the curtain. "See that big eye? That's the All-Seeing Eye. This is what this book says about that."

The eye, enveloped in a blaze of light and glory, reminds us that the scrutinizing gaze of the Omniscience is ever upon us; that all our thoughts, and words, and actions are open to His survey. He dwells in unapproachable light, and looketh kindly down upon man, providing for his wants; and in the minuteness of His care, numbers all the hairs on our heads. It is therefore our duty to live and act as under the eye of our All-seeing Judge, who will bring us into judgment for all our proceedings.

Theodora responded, "I don't understand what you're getting at."

"What I'm saying is, we must be accountable for our actions. See those bound rods on the curtain next to the skull and crossbones?" I asked. Theodora nodded. "Those bound rods symbolize strength in numbers. One rod alone could be broken, but together, as a group and bound together, they're difficult to break. As a group, the three of us can be a success in this endeavor—in any endeavor. We simply must stay together and be of one mind. It is through our numbers that we achieve our strength."

Theodora remained unmoved but asked, "So what's up with the heart and the hand?"

I got excited. "It symbolizes that whatever your actions may be, they must be guided by your heart, that your hand follows your heart. It means that when the Odd Fellow extends his hand, the welcome proceeds from the heart."

Theodora lifted herself in the chair and sat straighter.

"The one I like the best is the three links. According to Grosh, 'The three links remind us that the only chain by which we are bound together is that of Friendship, Love, and Truth; and that we are obligated, by the most sacred considerations, to violate neither of these principles.'"

I walked to my suitcase again and pulled from it a small eight-by-ten glass-covered frame holding a tattered sampler. At the top of the sampler were the words *Friendship and Love*. At the bottom were the words *and Truth*. Between these sets of words were two hands shaking with rays emanating from them. On both sides of the hands were the three links. I handed it to Theodora.

"This is one of my favorite possessions."

Mark walked into the room and lay down on my bed. He stared at the ceiling as he said, "So Joaquin pulled out the moth-eaten curtain."

I turned to Mark. "It's not moth-eaten."

Mark turned his head toward me ever so slightly; it was almost undetectable, but there was a sliver of a twinkle in his eyes as he looked at me.

In a less defensive tone I said, "The moth holes are barely noticeable." I paused before stating the reason for this entire conversation. "Mark and I would like you to become an Odd Fellow, or rather a Rebekah, the lady Odd Fellow. Would you consider it?"

Theodora had an uncomfortable, puzzled look on her face. It was only because of our friendship and history together that she even considered it, I'm sure.

"It isn't a cult, is it?" Theodora asked.

"No, of course not. I wouldn't belong to a cult and Mark is too surly to belong to a cult."

Mark nodded. "I'm too surly for a cult."

Theodora remained silent. We all remained silent. I walked over to the window and looked out. A slow rumbling moved throughout the room. There was just the slightest movement, the slightest rattling, and the slightest creaking.

Mark sat up and said, "Did you feel that? That was an earthquake!"

I stood in front of the Maximilian and Carlota window, listening. The only sound in the room came from the tinkling of some glass prisms clinking together in the light fixture above.

I could hear the creak of a door opening and then leather-soled footsteps in the hallway. They stopped outside my bedroom door. It was Lord Leighton.

"Hello, all," he said. "These temblors are most distressing."

"You felt it?" Mark asked.

Lord Leighton nodded yes.

"I think it was about a 5.0," said Mark.

"I am no expert or authority on such matters," Leighton said, "but they have become more frequent of late."

"Where's Mr. D?" I asked.

Mark turned his head toward me. "Sleeping downstairs."

Leighton walked into the room and saw the curtain. "Ah, I see you are part of the brotherhood of man."

Theodora used her index finger to point at Mark and me. She didn't move her hand. She merely moved her finger back and forth between the two of us with a motion similar to a windshield wiper. She mouthed the word "Odd."

Leighton laughed and informed us that he, too, was an Odd Fellow.

Mr. Dangerous lazily walked into the room and over to me. I picked him up and looked him in the eyes.

"Did you feel the earthquake?"

With eyes half-closed he barely looked awake and responded the way he often does; he looked around the room at everyone assembled in a leisurely and unhurried manner and then back to me and gave my cheek a slow, deliberate lick.

V.

MARK CROWDEN'S BLOG:
FRIENDSHIP, LOVE, AND TRUTH

I would walk naked—after being dipped in honey—through a hundred-foot flower-covered loggia *swarming* with irate bees for Joaquin—but I still resent him. Not in an angry or hateful way, but sometimes his quiet and steady temperament annoys the crap out of me.

Three years ago I wasn't drinking and I was still having difficulty walking. This wasn't the extent of my debility, though, because it gestated, progressed, and eventually it became a dilemma for me to walk up stairs. It culminated when I began to drag my left leg in an obvious and hideously embarrassing way. I certainly noticed myself doing this, but I clutched to my past good health and pretended it wasn't happening. I was able to proceed under this ruse for quite some time and could have continued to do so if it hadn't been for my friends and coworkers. For some reason they all felt it was appropriate to mention it, to bring it up and continue to talk about it, in depth, as I stared at them with a wide-eyed, hostile look upon my face. It is so frickin' pathetic to continue to deny something when person after person makes it the point of every single nostril-snorting, teeth-grinding, lip-chewing conversation. I am such a loser. After consulting with a specialist I came to understand how involved the surgery would be and how long my recovery would take. So because of the bigmouths, I finally underwent hip replacement surgery. Prior to my hospitalization Joaquin helped me adapt my home to the obstacles I would encounter post-surgery. The day the procedure took place he drove me to the hospital. While I was in the hospital he visited me daily and brought me items I needed. When I was released he drove me home. During my recuperation he bought groceries for me, made my meals, washed the dishes, mopped the kitchen, cleaned my bathroom, helped me in and out of the tub, helped me get dressed, made my bed, and ran errands for me. He did all of this willingly and never complained. You have no idea how much he ticks me off.

See, when that little weasel needs help he won't ask for any. He has a fierce determination to be independent. I suspect it has something to do with the fact that he spent his whole childhood as an orphan (no one ever adopted *him*) and never had anyone to rely on except himself, but it's so damn annoying to want to help someone, to pay them back, and they won't let you. Isn't that part of friendship? Theodora once said that in any relationship—whether it's between a mother and daughter, a husband and wife, or best friends—a whole part of the relationship is to make the other person miserable. I don't agree with that twisted statement, but let me tell you something, that little pansy-ass weasel Joaquin pisses me off.

How selfish and self-centered can he be? Doesn't he realize that I want to help him too? I long for the day when I will be able to help Joaquin, when I will extend my hand in friendship and he will not turn away.

❖

Even though I would never want to admit it, I *confess*, Joaquin's lack of "need" and individualistic nature has had an impact on my psyche. It has created Mongo confusion inside my head, much more so than the insane argument that took place the third day.

The day started with a temperamental outburst from Theodora and proceeded into an overwrought argument between her and Lord Leighton. Leighton very casually mentioned the brotherhood to Theodora while the two of them were standing on the porch.

He said something in the vein of "it would be to your advantage…"

Theodora then expressed her dislike for the religious aspects of the Odd Fellows, which I can certainly understand.

I walked out onto the veranda with my camera as she said, "I don't know if I can make that scene."

She was getting snappy as she smoked her cigarette, and this prompted me to yell over my shoulder for Joaquin. I mentioned to Theodora that even though I went to a Catholic boys' school in my youth I, too, had some issues with the Odd Fellows' overt embrace of Christianity. I stated that the school I attended was St. Lazarus. It was an extremely rigid place with Padre Tomas as our earthly leader and a flock of sisters to teach us. Our school emblem was a nun, dressed in her habit, with her fists up like a pugilist. Our motto: *God is with us.*

"Really, I understand how you feel," I said sincerely.

Well, Theodora didn't want to hear about my religious upbringing. It just perturbed her even more. She sighed loudly and gave me a look that said either *don't be condescending* or *F.U.* I get those two looks confused, and I should know the difference between them since I get them so often from so many different people.

When Leighton said something about "salvation and redemption" I realized all hope was lost for a prompt resolution to this situation. Theodora said she wasn't going to be force-fed "religious manure" by "middle-age lardos."

Ouch!

Then she used a series of expletives, directed at Leighton, which caused him to say, "You've no right to speak to me in that manner."

She said, "Listen to me, Little Lord Blueboy, I'll speak to you any way I want."

She threw her cigarette at him (what's with the cigarette throwing?) and stormed off into the house.

As Leighton and I watched the door slam he said, "One feels a massive Christian sympathy for her."

Theodora yelled back, *"I don't want your sympathy, you English asshole!"*

I turned to Leighton and whispered, "I must apologize. She's new at this concierge thing. It's on-the-job training for her, so we'll have to allow her a learning curve. I'll have Joaquin talk to her." I patted him on the shoulder as I said this.

He slowly turned his head toward me and said, "I don't like to be touched."

I'm surrounded by freaks.

With everyone's boundaries established, Leighton took

off his shoes and socks and went for a walk on the beach. I remained on the porch till Joaquin finally appeared. Mr. Dangerous followed him wearing a small, short, off-white cape attached to his collar. The cape covered his back region and had two Odd Fellows symbols and three letters, embroidered in blue thread, upon it. The first symbol was a cross. The second symbol was a dove, and the three letters were *F*, *L*, and *T*. I stared at Mr. Dangerous, who looked up at me.

"What is he wearing?" I asked.

Joaquin said he had made the cape for Mr. D. and did all the embroidery work himself. "I attached it to his collar with Velcro. Isn't it cool?"

I stared at Mr. D. "Cool? I don't know. Odd? Yes."

"Are you saying you don't like it?"

I shook my head as I smiled. Mr. D. had rushed off the porch and was running around on the lawn now, the cape fluttering out behind him as he ran. While we stood on the porch—watching Mr. D. and, farther off in the distance, Lord Leighton walking on the beach—I recounted what had happened earlier. I told Joaquin that he needed to speak to Theodora and tell her Lord Leighton had apologized.

"Maybe you could add something about how he becomes nervously dogmatic around attractive young women."

"Did he say that?" Joaquin asked.

"Well, no, but Theodora would probably forgive him if she thought it was because he felt nervous due to all her female allure."

"Why do I have to lie?" asked Joaquin.

"Well," I said as I patted him on the back, "it's because in the hoi polloi set we have become immersed in, no one thinks you ever will."

He did not respond.

"Now, getting back to Mr. D.'s cape—maybe you could make him a black cape just in case we take him to a fancy-dress function?"

Joaquin still did not respond, but I could tell the idea intrigued him. He looked out at Mr. Dangerous and I could tell he was imagining what a black cape would look like on him.

"If you use black fabric and then edge it in gold braid... with gold thread for the symbols? That would give Mr. D. a cosmopolitan look."

I nodded in an exaggerated manner to emphasize what I had said.

Joaquin stood next to me for a moment before he said, "Watch Mr. D. for me." Then he walked into the house.

I yelled back at him, "Remember to talk to Theodora before you start sewing."

That was easy.

I wondered what had happened to Señor De La Santos, since he seemed so confident. Maybe the car wasn't ready? I waited a few minutes on the porch and then ventured upstairs and hoped the Theodora conversation was over or almost over. I poked my head into Joaquin's room and found him sitting alone on his bed cutting up what appeared to be *my* black shirt. I hesitantly walked into the room.

"How did the tête-à-tête with Theodora go?"

"I didn't talk to her."

"Why not?"

"Because I'm not lying."

"What you doing?"

"Making a black cape for Mr. D." Joaquin looked up. "Where's Mr. Dangerous?"

"Outside."

Joaquin got up from the bed, picked up all his stuff, and walked past me. The only words emitted from his mouth were, "You're not supposed to leave him alone."

I walked next door to Theodora's room and knocked. She opened the door a crack. I could see and smell her smoke.

"Hi, Theodora," I said in super-charming mode.

"Cut the bullcrap, Mark. Joaquin told me you were coming up to tell me lies."

"That's *so* not true," I said.

"Whatever," she said, and slammed the door in my face.

As I turned around, in an almost inaudible voice, I said, "freak."

From the other side of the door Theodora yelled, *"I can hear you."*

Well, fiddle-dee-dee.

I walked downstairs and found Joaquin on the porch sewing. Mr. D. was chasing a butterfly around the porch. The butterfly was toying with him because at one point it led him along, across the entire length of the veranda, and then flew off. Mr. Dangerous looked up and, not paying attention, ran quickly and ended up flying off the porch with only a yelp before we heard a gooflike thud. After about a minute he reappeared at the stairs of the porch and ascended them, slightly dirty, and strangely I could detect a trace of humiliation attached to the dust on his fur and his cape.

Joaquin asked, "Are you all right?"

Mr. D. remorsefully walked up to Joaquin and sat at his feet. This allowed Joaquin the opportunity to bend over and kiss him on the head.

I stood there for the longest while in silence. I knew it was futile for me to bring up the Theodora/Leighton argument and the events that had ensued, since all Joaquin did was prevent me from forcing him into a lie, and anyway, he probably wouldn't discuss it. When Joaquin doesn't want to discuss something he always says, "I decline to argue." The rancor that rises up within me when he says that is almost grotesque, and I often feel as if my head will burst into a million pieces. Most times I don't even want to argue, but then he'll say, "I decline to argue," at which point I know the matter is resolved as far as he is concerned. So even if I wanted to argue, I couldn't. Which is another thing he does that annoys me. I need to start making a list of everything he does that annoys me. Make a mental note: buy a notepad.

Lord Leighton appeared on the porch and didn't say anything when he saw Joaquin sewing or Mr. D. in a cape. I thought it was astute of him and figured he, at least, had learned something from the Theodora confrontation. Before he went inside he said he wanted to speak to both of us later that day regarding a very important matter that involved our immortal souls. Ay-ay-ay. If he turns out to be some religious fanatic, his English butt is out of here, and let me tell you something, I will decline to argue about it with anyone.

En la tarde, Mr. De La Santos arrived and brought not only bad news but both good and bad karma. Theodora was still holed up in her room smoking cigarettes and drinking Dr Pepper, like a nicotine-addicted version of Agnes Gooch, so in that big oversized foyer De La Santos gave Joaquin, Mr. D., and me the bad news: our SUV had been stolen!

The three of us remained frozen for about ten seconds till Joaquin loudly exclaimed, "Oh, no! This is a catastrophe. What are we going to do now?"

It was then Mr. D. started barking, chasing his tail in a

circle and making himself dizzy. Joaquin continued to talk nonstop about how unfortunate this state of events was and how we hadn't planned on the purchase of a new vehicle.

I thought, maybe, Joaquin should calm down and not get overly excited so I said, "You might take it down a notch, Joaquin."

He stared at me with an aggrieved look and said, "Mark, maybe you don't understand, but this is disastrous. That SUV was our link to the outside world. Those donkeys are not the easiest way to get around."

Mr. D. stopped chasing his tail and stumbled around like he was drunk. I told Mr. D. to "stop that."

"Don't yell at him," said Joaquin.

Mr. De La Santos looked at the three of us like we were crazy Americanos.

I caught Mr. De La Santos's eyes and mouthed the words, "I'm not with them."

Joaquin pulled a spool of thread out of his pocket and threw it at my head; it hit me above the right ear.

"Ow!"

As I rubbed my head, Joaquin asked Mr. De La Santos what the chances were of getting our SUV back and De La Santos laughed and said there was always a *"poquito"* chance. He then said he wanted to move in...*here*...and not pay rent.

My reaction was, "What?"

He smiled as if he understood my puzzlement to his request. He very confidently stated there were "banditos" throughout the region and it might be a good idea to have a local amigo under the roof. Plus, he had transportation. He pointed toward his car through the window. I took short steps and crouch-walked *almost* over to the window. I peered out at a car that appeared to be a 1967 Chevy Impala convertible. So, not only was he bandito repellent, but he had a cool ride, too. The three of us had a quick powwow.

"What do you think, Joaquin?"

Joaquin smiled and nodded vigorously.

I looked down at Mr. D. "What do you think, D-dog?"

Mr. Dangerous barked three times in the affirmative.

I extended my hand to Mr. De La Santos and said, "I say yes, too. Do you have any luggage? Joaquin can get it out of your car for you."

Mr. De La Santos didn't respond, but I still clapped my hands twice and simultaneously said to Joaquin, "Chop chop."

I'm glad Joaquin didn't have another spool of thread in his pocket 'cause he gave me a look that wasn't too friendly.

That was the good karma. The bad karma was De La Santos strongly urged us *not* to buy the property. If we had to have it, *if we could not be dissuaded,* he urged us to lease it for a year or possibly six months.

"Don Humberto wants the papers signed, and the money transferred, as quickly as possible," said De La Santos.

I asked the obvious question of "Why?" Why didn't he want us to buy the property outright? He wasn't explaining. He bit his lip and looked from side to side. Joaquin was holding Mr. D. and both leaned in with confused looks on their faces. Mr. Dangerous made a quizzical sound that, I swear to God, sounded like "What?" (He is the smartest dog ever.) Mr. De La Santos said he didn't want to talk about it. Mary, mother of Jesus—I've got another Joaquin on my hands!

"Unless you explain what you're holding back," I said, "we're buying it. So spit it out, man."

De La Santos opened his mouth hesitantly. The three of us

were transfixed on his lips but they didn't move. He seemed to be suffering from some sort of male hysteria that prevented the words from coming out.

"What is it?" I asked.

De La Santos closed his lips. He stared straight ahead and we all turned around when he pointed at something behind us.

Lord Leighton walked into the foyer. In a loud voice that echoed off the walls and staircase, Leighton said, "Desperation and regret is what awaits you if you remain in this house."

I looked at De La Santos, who refused to look at me. I shifted my gaze to Joaquin, who appeared tense. Uneasiness crossed over his face. Mr. Dangerous felt Joaquin's fear because he began to shake and laid his little ears back on his head timidly.

Leighton walked farther into the room and said, "It is the Chupacabras and death that await you here. Death cannot be undone. If you choose to stay, you must make it your duty to destroy the Chupacabras. We must be united in this. Do you understand?"

I stood silently with an exasperated look on my face.

"What the H are you talking about?" I asked.

"Señor De La Santos knows," said Leighton. "He is aware of the mysteries that encircle this evil force. He is so wary of the evil that gestates and then springs forth from this monster that he cannot even speak of it. *Death* to you, *death* to Joaquin, *death* to Miss Russell, *death* to Señor De La Santos, and *death* to your little French bulldog—that is what the future holds."

Mr. D., still shaking, let out a tiny yelp as he blinked his eyes. De La Santos looked angry as he took Leighton's comments as some sort of English affront to his third-world manhood.

"I feel obligated to speak the unmitigated and indelicate truth before I urge you to sign the papers and take possession of this house immediately," said Leighton.

"There is no such creature as the Chupacabras," I said, knowing full well that only yesterday I had claimed to have seen it.

"Ah, denial is one avenue to take," said Leighton as he nodded. "Rest assured, my good man, there is such a being and it walks the earth. The Chupacabras can be stopped and killed, but you must enter into this endeavor with both eyes open. You speak only realms of fiction when you deny its existence. The divine gift of life is worth fighting for, and I ask you to join me in that fight."

My head shook back and forth. It moved without any prodding from me. "I don't understand," I said. "Why are you here?"

I moved closer to Leighton and stared directly into his face. As if channeling the strength of Atlas, he looked just as strongly back, but unlike Atlas he abruptly averted his gaze. He moved away from the four of us. His footsteps sounded loud and empty on the hard floor.

His back was to me as I said, "I demand to know why you're here. Why you wanted to be our first guest."

"Now, mate," Leighton said as he turned around, "there's no reason to glare. There's no reason to be suspicious. This is no time for a bust-up. We've all had a lovely time together and got on so well."

I stood looking at him. There was a tiny bead of perspiration traveling down the side of his face; it went from his temple to his jawline. What he said wasn't true.

He continued, "It would be a lie to say I don't have nefarious motives. I do. I came here deliberately. Not because the place suited my fancy—not in the way you're attracted to it. I came here because of its location, because of its proximity to the house on the hill."

He raised his arm and pointed his finger toward what I could only describe then as the unknown. Light filtered through the stained-glass windows that frame that immensely overdone staircase, and illuminated his hand. It reminded me of a neon sign, pointing—directing us.

Leighton walked to the farthest edge of the foyer, turned back, and said, "Reported attacks began to be documented in the nineties, first in Puerto Rico and then in Moca. A series of attacks occurred in San Antonio, Coleman, and Cuero, Texas. All of these attacks involved the sucking of blood from livestock. Subsequent investigations deemed that most of the carcasses found and examined, and I repeat the words *found* and *examined*, were deemed by 'authorities' to be coyotes with severe cases of mange. Now, I ask you gentlemen, when did the public start believing the authorities again? In my estimation the public stopped believing them sometime after 1963."

Leighton walked back to us and stood an arm's length away as he continued. "Most authorities talk the most awful rubbish. Only the most gullible believe any of them. I suspect, because of the Internet, we have entered the age of the anti-authority."

Leighton turned to me. He brushed the sleeves of his shirt as if attempting to brush away lint that didn't exist before he looked up and asked, "What do you think, Mr. Crowden?"

I caught Leighton's eye for a second and then deliberately turned back to the "three of them" and winked.

For everyone to hear and for Leighton in particular, I said loudly, "You're scaring the dog."

Mr. D. barked and tried to wiggle out of Joaquin's arms.

Leighton squinted his eyes as he looked at me. I used the nail on my middle finger to scratch one of my front teeth. I stopped scratching and looked at my nail. The room remained silent. I looked up and took a step toward Leighton.

I whispered into his ear, "Stop talking hogwash."

VI.
THEODORA RUSSELL'S DIARY: THE DISAPPEARANCE

Alakazam. One tantrum and, suddenly, they're all walking around whispering. What little brainpower those idiots possessed was individually and collectively tightly wrapped around the one element that gets men to stick together—fear. Fear of a female. Those bastards were afraid my bad aura would explode and land on them like alien venom. I love it when that happens. Little Lord Blueboy and all his revolting grossness didn't travel into town with us. He stayed locked in his room poring over old books and damaged newspaper clippings. He used a large tortoiseshell magnifying glass to look at things. It was ginormous, almost the size of a dinner plate.

He would chew on a pencil while he read and every few moments say "fiddle-faddle" while he nodded like a silly bobble-headed toy.

I'm glad he caught me spying. Most people would see it as a giant fail, but I don't care. Go ahead—close the door. I've got better things to do than spy on some English chubster with a big third eye. When he bolted the lock shut I figured *he's probably in love with me already.* I need to tell that pompous ugly prig I don't give a rat's ass what he thinks.

❖

De La Santos put the top down and we jumped in; Joaquin, who was wearing a ball cap advertising his alma mater, sat with me in the back. Mark and the frog dog (wearing a frickin' cape!) rode shotgun. De La Santos peeled out and kicked up a cloud of dust that caused Joaquin to cough dramatically.

I sneered at him, pulled out a cigarette, and lit up. De La Santos drives crazy, like Death's chasing him with an overdue IOU. Man, he might think about putting on the brakes once in a while because Mexico isn't gonna live much longer if he keeps driving like that.

We were headed back to Felipe so the high-toned bear and the Holy One could sign the lease. They had decided not to buy it outright and instead lease it for a year. I tried not to roll my eyes when Fatboy told me about the decision. Hey, it's not my moolah, but I still wish they would have consulted me before changing the plan. They acted so smug, patting each other on the shoulder like it was the right thing to do. Whatever. Jerks.

We hurtled like a cannonball up to the land agent's office and stopped so quickly it threw everyone's head forward and then back. As the dust settled I realized we had arrived. There should have been an attendant beside the Impala lifting up the ride's bar and helping me out, but there wasn't, so I stumbled out disoriented. I felt as if I had smoked a bad cigarette that made me light-headed.

De La Santos opened the front door of his office and we trudged in and plopped down on some worn, green vinyl sofas that had a vintage look. There were venetian blinds on the windows that hadn't been dusted in a long time, and old 1960s travel posters hung on the walls advertising Mexico City, Acapulco, and Rosarita. The posters had faded so much the destinations didn't look enticing anymore. I have no desire to travel to a place where everything is a whitish-yellow color. Not my scene.

De La Santos went to an old refrigerator and pulled out four bottles of orange Fanta. He needed a bottle opener to remove the bottle caps. He opened a bottle and gave it to Joaquin, who immediately asked for some water for his mutt. Mexico sat the other bottles down on the coffee table in front of me and handed me the bottle opener.

As he walked off I sat staring at Joaquin, Mr. D., and Mark with a look on my face that said, "Ladies don't open their own bottles."

I wasn't successful conveying my *lady-ness* because Mark looked at me with his head slightly tilted and said, "Joaquin's thirsty, Theodora. Could you speed it up?"

He grabbed Joaquin's Fanta bottle and took a swig.

"Ah," he said loudly.

Then he did that thing he does with his index finger; he points it at you and then twirls it in a clockwise motion real fast.

That Mark Crowden is a real bitch. Shove that twirling finger up your big ass, Vandyke-y.

It was hot and stagnant in the room. De La Santos turned

on a radio but he kept the volume down low so the sound was just loud enough to fill the empty void our lack of conversation created. Joaquin's mutt was our only diversion. He coaxed him into doing a series of tricks so the pooch rolled over, sat, begged, and was just about to eagerly play dead when a car drove up. It sat idling outside. Mexico got up and walked to the door, which he opened and then motioned for the person to come in. No one exited the vehicle. The only response he received was when a back window rolled down a sliver of a crack. It was a huge, long, old lumbering vehicle with tinted windows—waxed up real pretty to look new even though it had to be from the 1920s or '30s.

Peering through one of the venetian blinds, I watched as De La Santos walked down to the vehicle, but he quickly took a step back. I could see his mouth move but couldn't hear what he said. Some papers slid through the window's crack and Santos gingerly took them, turned around, and walked back into the office.

"It's Don Humberto," he said. "*No quiere entrar*. He wants you to sign the papers. He doesn't want to come in."

Mark cocked his head to the side and I watched as his eyes looked up and then slowly moved completely around their sockets.

"That's strange," Mark said, "We want to meet him."

Joaquin and D-Dog's heads moved in unison, listening to what Mexico and Mark said, looking from one to the other.

"Maybe you should just sign *los papeles*?"

Mark walked up to Mexico and took the papers from his extended hand. Fatboy examined the contract and proclaimed it to be a standard two-page lease right before he handed it to Joaquin.

"Should we go out to the car?" Mark asked. "We would like to say hello."

Mexico seemed distracted. He kept looking over his shoulder at the car idling outside. At the same time he seemed to brush off Mark's suggestion with a shrug and told 'em both to sign the papers and we could walk out to the vehicle.

As Joaquin looked at Mark, he held a pen dramatically poised to sign. His arm was raised high, his elbow was crooked, and the pen was rigidly and eagerly held in his hand. The wigged dudes who signed the Declaration of Independence didn't use as much dramatic flair as Joaquin was using at this moment. He addressed Mark when he said, "This will only lead to trouble—you realize that?"

Mark responded by making a statement I also didn't understand. He nodded and said, "It doesn't exist."

What is this? Are they talking in oddball code?

Joaquin stared at Mark for three or four seconds before he signed the lease. He handed the lease and pen to Mark, who hurriedly signed it, and voilà! It was back in Mexico's hands.

Mexico looked the papers over, swallowed something stuck in his throat, and glanced at us with a strained look on his face.

"Vente." He used his head to direct us to the door.

We walked out into the morning sun, down the steps, and to the car. We didn't get too close because a funky stench came from the window's crack.

Mexico stood closest to the vehicle as he said, "Don Humberto, let me introduce Señores Crowden and Moreno and Señorita Russell, and their little *perro.*"

Mexico pointed to Mr. D. down at Joaquin's feet. D-Dog

let out a tiny yelp, turned around, and ran back into the office. That dog's a pussy.

No response came from Don Humberto. Mexico slid the lease through the window's crack. I could see only the tips of four gray, bony fingers. Without a word the window closed. The windows were tinted, but it still appeared as if no one was driving the car. I should have been able to see at least a shape in the driver's seat, but I could see none. The car pulled away and was quickly all over the road, menacingly going from one side to the other. Holy moly! Apparently, it was being driven by a madman. It suddenly jerked to a stop, paused, and then did a screeching donut in the middle of the street before heading back toward us—*fast!* We ran to the doorway of the land office and watched as the car sped past us, backfired, and came to a stop. It sat idling for the longest time, prompting me to think someone would exit and immediately pass out in the street, but no one did. Instead, the psycho car did a series of hydraulic lifts—up and down, up and down—before it sped off and disappeared into a cloud of its own dust.

That certainly didn't roll as expected.

Mark said to no one in particular, "We're in business with that man now." He threw his arms up in the air in an exasperated manner before he tapped Joaquin on the shoulder, leaned in, and whispered, "Say a prayer for us."

The arms in the air bit was the first of three clichéd acts I would witness this day. Mark says witnessing three clichéd acts in a single day is a bad sign and an omen that the end of civilization as we know it could possibly be here. Not definitely here, but possibly here. So, clichéd acts are conditional apocalyptic signs? Yes, I know it makes no sense, but that's what the big buffoon claims, and outlandish, flaky statements are often the ones that are the most memorable.

❖

Big Boy wanted to go shopping. He said he wanted to buy a notepad, so we walked over to a large *mercado* that sold fresh fish, bootleg DVDs, chorizo, Fanta, and other crap. Joaquin attempted to help Mark select a notepad, but Mark snarled at every single one Joaquin held up for approval. Joaquin should have known Mark wouldn't want a lame notepad with a kitten or unicorn on the cover. Every time he held one up Mark scowled. It was obvious Mark was infuriated and wanted to throw a notepad at Joaquin, but he resisted. That Joaquin is smart. He knows when to carry that pooch. Mark finally selected a huge five-subject, five-hundred-page notebook with a cover of a dinosaur eating a lamb. Blood dripped from the lamb's mouth. I'm not sure it was historically accurate, but I kept my trap shut.

It was after this that it happened.

I was walking with Mexico in the *mercado*. Mark and Joaquin were following us, not directly behind us but near enough. Joaquin carried Mr. D. and everything seemed kissy. I could hear music in the distance and the murmur of voices everywhere. The day was pleasant as far as those things go (and no one had annoyed me in the past ten minutes) when a slow rumbling overtook the place; that rumbling quickly turned into outright shaking—violent shaking. Stuff from above us fell to the ground and merchandise flew off the tables in five thousand different directions. I turned back to see Mark push Joaquin and D-Dog under some large tables, and as if in slow motion, he crawled under the table himself. I fell into Mr. De La Santos and he fell onto me as I fell backward onto a table. It was then that I saw a crazy-ass dude with a guitar hurl toward Mexico. It happened in an instant. I definitely saw a switchblade headed toward Mexico's neck. He was going to shank him! The switchblade sparkled in the light but then the guitar dude lost his footing and the switchblade came down and sliced Mexico's arm instead. Blood squirted out. A look of pain crossed De La Santos's face as I screamed. There were screams coming from everywhere. They continued as long as the shaking. When it stopped there was silence and a momentarily stillness until the dude with the guitar jumped up and took off. I could hear his footsteps running away on the concrete floor.

De La Santos's face contorted as he tried to hold in his pain.

I looked at him for a second before I slapped him hard on the cheek and yelled, "Scream!"

Good Lord. I could feel *hombre* tears bubbling up. He exhaled a loud sound of pain and I held him as his body went limp.

Could any part of this situation suck more? Is it possible?

People ran from the building as aftershocks shook the place. The three of *them* climbed out from underneath the tables. Joaquin and D-Dog looked scared; both had big eyes, and Mr. D's ears were back and flat on his head while Joaquin's ball cap was ajar—pimp daddy style.

Mark, on the other hand, acted like a man about town on his way to a highbrow party; he had a big smile on his face. He looked excited. He was sprucing himself up, rearranging his shirt, making sure his buttons were buttoned, that sort of thing—until his eyes zeroed in on Mexico's bloody arm.

He was all business as he swiftly attended to it. It wasn't nearly as bad as I first imagined, more of a surface wound than an emergency room wound. Mark, cocksure as ever, bandaged it up with a quick professionalism.

The street outside was in a Mexican jumping-bean panic. Confused señoritas and wrong-way señors ran in every direction in mass hysteria, and while they might have had specific destinations in mind, I swear a number of the same people ran past me more than once. They were marauding nuisances. I longed for a big needle filled with a magic potion, preferably idiot retardant, so I could stab the misdirected over and over and over again and put an end to their torment of me. According to fancy-pants Mark, "some of the vernacular buildings" stood up quite well to the earthquake while others were but rubble. It was only a few blocks to Mexico's office, so we shuffled down the street because the sidewalk was too susceptible to falling objects. Mexico had no difficulty walking but he didn't appreciate it when some running fool bumped into his bandaged arm, and the street was full of running fools. Mark finally walked beside him, protecting him. He was a big American shield.

His office was still standing when we arrived, and he crossed himself while looking up to heaven when he saw this. It was behavior beneath him and the second clichéd act I would witness this day. Getting through the front door was a task because the doorjamb had shifted, but Mark managed to push it open through the utter force of his weight. Mexico told us all to follow him into the back office. It was barren except for a cheap bed and dresser, a chair with chipped paint, and an old book about the 1960s supermodel Twiggy on the floor. In the corner of the room was a locked closet. Is a locked closet ever a good thing? Locked closets are for dead bodies, porn, and precisely what Mexico had stashed inside this one. While he went through the motions of unlocking it he said we were going to need "these" right before the final twist and click. The "these" he spoke of were guns, lots of guns. It was an arsenal worthy of Scarface. There must have been a hundred different guns, rifles, and shotguns. It was bulging with firearms and boxes and boxes of ammo.

What kind of man is he?

Mark and Joaquin looked from the guns to him apprehensively.

De La Santos explained and didn't explain when he said in an offhanded way, "They were here when I moved in."

I stared at him with a distrusting face. He expected us to buy that explanation hook, line, and sinker?

Mexico told Mark to stick out his arms, but Mark didn't. He stood motionless. De La Santos said, "You know we're going to need these."

Mark still didn't respond. While he remained unco-operative, Joaquin silently walked up like an obedient child and put his arms out. De La Santos started piling rifles across Joaquin's arms. He fished in his pocket for his keys, tossed them to me, and told me to open the trunk of the Impala. I didn't move. Mexico looked at me. My lack of movement upset him.

With an agitated look on his face and blood seeping from his bandage, he barked, "Now!"

I don't normally take orders from men, but I made an exception in this case.

Joaquin and I were stacking and then restacking rifles in the trunk to get them to fit when Mark appeared in the land office doorway. He was carrying shotguns that had awkwardly fanned out and he was attempting to get them into some manageable state. He walked down onto the steps and shouted at the three of us.

"Hey! De La Santos is filling up an orange crate with handguns and ammo. Somebody go get it."

I looked at big Mark for a second and decided I was back to not taking orders from men.

As I shuffled the rifles in the trunk I whispered under my breath, "Ladies don't carry crates filled with guns."

Joaquin looked down at Mr. D., who was sniffing the dirt, and said, "Come on, D-Dog, let's go get a crate of guns!"

Mr. D. barked and ran up the steps as Mark descended them.

When we finished loading our arsenal, the trunk would barely close. Some of the shotguns were stacked in the backseat where Mexico and I sat. Mark drove, and D-Dog and Joaquin sat up front with him.

It was a bitch of a day. It was insinuated that I was a spy, I was almost run over by my new landlord, I saw my future boyfriend slashed during an earthquake, and I helped stack guns in the back of a 1967 Impala. This bed-and-breakfast gig was turning out to not be the wisest career move. I'm not digging it.

The chubster with the third eye was waiting on the veranda when we came back. Mark drove straight across the grass, past the Mexican palms, past the plants and stinkweed, and right up to the front porch. Little Lord Blueboy, who hadn't shaved and was all scruffy, was drinking an iced tea. He had placed a pitcher, with enough glasses for the rest of us, on a wicker table near the front door. He even had a bowl of cold water for Mr. Dangerous.

That pooch liked that. He lapped it up quickly and used his tongue to lick off all the excess water from his whiskers before he lay down for a nap at Mark's and my feet.

Mark and Mexico recounted all the circus top events of

the day, and as I listened I watched Leighton react. He looked like a gentleman hobo at a holiday mission feast. He gobbled up everything offered with a surprising and tasteful English dignity. We found ourselves laughing on the porch as the light from inside trickled out. As a bonus Mark decided to shoot the shiz, for the benefit of Leighton and De La Santos, and tell his crazy dog story. Throughout the retelling Joaquin tried to steer the yarn back to a realistic ending, but once Big Boy started slinging it, all any of us could do was sit back and let it hit us over the head.

With a loud "Well!" he began. He was all revved up and barely able to control himself.

"It was when Joaquin had just gotten Mr. D. and he was still a puppy. D-Dog, of course, immediately fell in love with me from the moment he saw me—which is understandable, as I'm sure all of you can attest to."

Mark nodded at all of us around the table. Joaquin smiled a melancholy smile like he had just seen a dead sparrow while De La Santos and Leighton looked on with confused faces, which made perfect sense. I bit down on my cigarette and inhaled.

"Anyway," Mark continued, "D-Dog liked being walked by me more than anyone else, since we looked so great walking down the street together. I swear, buds and budette, we were a male version of Ann Miller and the hounds in *Easter Parade*."

Mark lifted his head up, pushed out his chin, and puffed out his chest. My take on his poseur behavior was that numb-nuts was attempting to look high-class. When he spoke I realized I was in the general area but still wrong.

He said, "My good looks *oooozzzzed* over D-Dog and topped him off like a gas tank."

D-Dog noticeably grunted right at that moment and moved his little legs.

Mark looked down at him. "Hey, no interrupting my story."

He turned his attention back to the rest of us and looked around the table to make sure we all understood, and encouraged us to be properly engrossed by shaking his head and using crazy eyes to alert us to its importance. "Well, on this particular day we went to the LA River."

He stopped and said as an aside, "The LA River is this big concrete canal with a little bit of water, lots of trash, a spattering of foliage, and an occasional street person."

He said it in a dismissive way as if the location wasn't necessarily important but he was mentioning it merely to describe the backdrop for his big scene. Who does he think he is? The LA River is not the Nile.

He continued, "So, I had momentarily let Mr. D. off his leash, and what did that puppy dog immediately do?"

Mark threw his right arm out and almost knocked over a glass, but the lug didn't stop to right it. Instead he said, "Mr. D. took off straight for this guy sitting down on a ledge near the water. The guy had his legs crossed, like a girl, and was wearing clogs. Yes, clogs. *Clogs*, of all things!"

When he said *clogs*, he had a repulsed look on his face. The corner of one lip moved up in a snarl like a dog on the verge of barking. It was apparent he couldn't imagine any man ever wearing clogs for any reason, at any time, anywhere.

"Uh, we were in Los Angeles, not Heidi's Nordic-land," he said.

Joaquin interjected, "Wasn't Heidi from Switzerland?"

Mark held up his finger and said, "You're interrupting my story, GPS boy."

Joaquin put his hand over his mouth.

"Anyway," Mark continued, "so now we had to walk down and talk to Clogs, who was putting his funky hands all over Mr. D's fur."

Joaquin interrupted again. "Clogs was a kook."

Everybody looked at Joaquin. Mark squinted his eyes and pointed at Joaquin with a shaky finger. Joaquin looked away quickly and took a sip of his tea through a straw.

The douche began again. "So, Clogs told us a long, long, long, long story about Molly Ringwald, how he once saw her, how he continually wrote her letters, how she never wrote him back, that kind of thing. Stalker stuff. As someone whose personality and body is le pussynip to le mad stalker, I know all about stalkers."

Mark paused before he continued. "Okay, he might have been borderline kooky, but I contend he was kooky only because his story went on so long and was meandering."

I exhaled some smoke and whispered, "Was it painfully long like this one?"

Mark reached out and touched my shoulder with the tip of a finger as he glared at me. "You've almost found my last cotton-pickin' nerve, lady."

I smiled at him, showing all my teeth, which prompted him to mimic me. Have I mentioned he's a dick? He needs to STFU.

Mark brought his story to the end of the line when he said, "At this point I smiled a big smile in Clogs' direction and said, *I'm sure your letters have created a sensation in Molly's home.*"

Mark stopped. He held out both hands in front of himself and jazzy hands shook them before us. He took a deep breath and spat out the payoff, "Then Clogs said, *It takes me a thousand words to say what you can say with one smile.*"

Mark threw his arms up in the air like a referee at a football game and smiled from ear to ear. "Isn't that sweet? Isn't that the sweetest thing you've ever heard from a guy wearing clogs?"

From across the table Joaquin said, "Clogs was a kook."

Mark shot a look at Joaquin, who quickly sipped his iced tea and pretended to be completely engrossed in the contents of his glass.

"That's a possibility, my sugary little churro."

Joaquin refused to leave it alone. He didn't look at the clog hater. He concentrated on his beverage and said, "You know, that line is probably from a Molly Ringwald movie."

Mark jumped up with a great deal of agility, considering he's a jumbo. He grabbed Joaquin around the chest, pulled him up, and carried him backward away from the table as Joaquin halfheartedly struggled and squealed, which quickly turned into laughing and giggling when Mark began twirling in circles, which made them both frickin' dizzy. The tipoff was the mutual staggering when Mark stopped. The staggering was followed by wrestling and Mark threatening to sit on Joaquin if he didn't take back the kook statement, and then Mark held Joaquin by his ankles and shook him, up and down, over the veranda's railing. The contents of Joaquin's pockets fell out—a spool of thread, change, a 1962 World's Fair key chain, a pack of tiny-size Chiclets, and a two-dollar bill. Joaquin once compared Mark to a carnival ride and Joaquin, God help his little Mexican soul, likes the carnival.

While the little pipsqueak may appear respectable, he still has a creepy and morbid side. For years Joaquin had a fascination with a particular painting, but he wouldn't tell anyone what it was and wouldn't let anyone see it. Because he's part of the opposite sex I expected it to be an explicit, lewd nude by a messed-up male artist. He would sit in a lonely fashion and stare at the image in one of his art books. His demeanor while viewing it was just shy of catatonic. The painting in question was his secret, and he would slam the book shut in an obvious and childish way whenever anyone walked into the room. Dude, just stop that.

A few months ago when I was in a detective mood, or maybe it was a pissy mood; anyway, whatever kind of mood it was, the mood launched me on the road to *WTF is that little freak looking at* so I crept up behind him and peeked over his shoulder. He immediately closed the book, but I still saw it. Using his shoulder as a wall, he turned and looked up at me in a defensive manner.

I bent over so I was up in his grill when I asked, "Would you like to explain that?" I tried not to look too disgusted.

He didn't 'fess up right away. In a detached manner he stood up and moved away from me, unsure where to go. When he was safely across the room he stood next to a bronze statue of an Indian scout he likes and used the fingers on his right hand to remove some of its dust.

It was only after he examined his dusty hand that he looked up and after some stuttering and stammering said, "It shows a new way to live."

I did not respond. I thought about what he had said and considered my response. He continued to look at his dusty hand and the conclusion I came to was *Yikes! What does that mean?* Jeez, I wish I hadn't peeked. I should have known better. I'm not cool with it, but getting all self-righteous and lecturing him endlessly would be troubling for me. Plus, there are larger issues involved here. Being a raving bitch wouldn't produce the desired result, so I figured screw it. I needed to make peace with it whether I wanted to or not.

The painting in question was one of those spooky, death-filled images of a lunatic woman who's so overcome with love and grief that she does the unimaginable. In the painting she's eating her husband's ashes after his cremation. Is that not loony? Joaquin told me later it was some nineteenth-century painting by some Italian guy whose name I can't remember.

I'm not sure if the Big Oaf knows but Joaquin should keep it a secret 'cause the B.O. would find it weird and s-c-a-r-y. I certainly find it troubling.

That nasty old Fauntleroy made a statement that made me laugh as the night turned from dusk to darkness. I mentioned casually the farm-girl entertainers we met during our thumbed ride and the other pack of ladies outside the Hacienda de Pleasure. I described their size 14+ bodies, their sturdy torsos, their shapely legs, their large breasts, their hefty arms, their huge heads, and their even huger hair. Not that there's anything wrong with their shapes, mind you, I simply wanted to make it clear what type of women they were. The old skeeve's response to me was not how unfortunate these woman's lives were *or* the injustice and gender politics involved *or* how they were being taken advantage of by *the man*, but instead that pervy perv from England turned his head at an angle and very mischievously said, "They sound rather dishy. Where *exactly* is this Hacienda again?"

I would have brained that old coot if I hadn't been laughing so much.

About a half hour later a full moon rose and illuminated the sky and landscape. I went inside. I was in my bedroom, writing in my diary, when Joaquin knocked on the door.

I didn't open it; his voice was muffled and I'm not really sure I heard him correctly, but it sounded like he said he needed me to try something on, to come to his room and bring high heels if I had any.

I didn't know what he was up to, but at this point I knew I had to "adapt," so I walked to his room in a bra, panties, and white high heels.

When Joaquin saw me he said, "Perfect! I want you to try something on."

Sheesh. I'm glad I brought my diary because I ended up doing a lot of writing. He asked me to stand on "this box." It was the orange crate that De La Santos had put the guns in. Then he pulled from his closet a white silken robe. It had a large quilted collar with quilted cuffs and an unfinished hem that was pinned. It also had some of those Odd Fellow symbols on it. Different symbols were embroidered in a copper-gold thread around the bottom of the garment, above the unfinished hem. There was also a large All-Seeing Eye on the left side where a pocket would normally be on a man's sports jacket. Across the back were the three links.

"I want you to put this on," he said. "I'm making it for myself, but if you wear heels you'll be about my height. I want to get the hem straight." He nodded and asked, "Okay?"

I sighed and looked around the room for a way to escape.

"Please," he said with a pinched-up face similar to one of those little beggar boys at the border.

"Jeez, Joaquin, I've been on my feet all day long. Have a little mercy."

I was reluctant to do it, but the day had been so troubling that finally I realized how important each one of these morons was to me. Maybe if I wasn't always fighting with them I could enjoy their company and the fact that we're friends? Maybe if

I wasn't always cutting people off at the knees, people would treat me the way I wanted to be treated?

I condensed these thoughts into nine words: "Don't have a nervous collapse, you fussy little schnook."

Joaquin put his index finger and thumb up to his lips, clasped them together, and turned them as if he was locking his lips shut. The third clichéd act of the day. I wanted to backhand him on the forehead.

"Give it to me." I tore the robe from him and put it on as he went to the closet and pulled out what I discovered in seconds to be a matching belt.

"Here, tie it with this," he said as he handed it to me.

I put it around my waist and tied it on the side. He stepped back and looked at me with his mouth half-opened.

"What?" I asked.

He smiled and walked over to a large cheval mirror sitting in the corner of the room. It matched all the other furniture in the room. A gay man must have decorated this place.

As he laboriously dragged it over he said, "Look at yourself."

He stopped and stood next to the mirror as I gazed at my reflection.

"You look like a bride."

He sounded like he was spinning a line of gold, but he was right. I did look like a bride. All I needed was a veil and De La Santos on my arm and I could get married in the church of the Odd Fellows. I don't know why I thought that. What a strange thing to pop into my head. And why did he have a book about Twiggy in his room?

Joaquin spent the longest time working on the hem; it had to be at least half an hour. I was getting impatient, which he must have realized from my constant fidgeting, loud sighing, and the glares I lasered at him. I was just about to call for a time-out when there was a crash downstairs.

"Where's Mr. D.?" Joaquin asked.

I looked behind me and there, on the bed, was D-Dog. The distant crash hadn't even budged him from his dog nap.

"He's asleep on the bed behind me."

"Well, I'm going downstairs to see what's up," Joaquin said. "We'll do some more tomorrow?"

He searched my face for some affirmation. I didn't want to commit verbally, so I nodded because I didn't want to see any muchacho tears tonight.

"Come on, Mr. D. We're going downstairs."

Mr. D. lifted his head off the bed sleepily. He looked backward over his shoulder with only a slight amount of interest. Joaquin clapped his hands together twice. The pooch knew what that meant. He got up, yawned, and walked to the edge of the bed. He hesitantly jumped down and followed Joaquin out into the hallway. His toenails clicked on the wood floor.

I stood on the crate looking at myself in the mirror. I'll never get married, I suspect. If I do, I don't plan on having a quilted collar and quilted cuffs on my wedding dress. That would be a mistake, and this is definitely the wrong color. I turned around on the crate to see the back and those darn rings. Friendship, love, and truth; the *Odds* seem to think that's what life's about. But aren't there other things? Shouldn't happiness get a ring? And death? Shouldn't there be a fourth ring for death? As I looked at myself in the mirror, I heard what sounded like gunshots. When I stepped down from the orange crate, I heard the strangest sound outside the door.

VII.
Joaquin Moreno's Journal: The Crucifixion

Through the smashed and broken window frame, the four of us stood and watched as Theodora was taken away. The full moon lit up the landscape and gave us a clear view. She was on her back and her arms were stretched out away from her body. Two large beasts, on all fours, carried her to the north. Each had one of her wrists in its mouth, their sharp teeth clamped down tight; her body was carried upon their backs. The white robe fluttered in the wind. Her hair swirled around her expressionless, trancelike face and she was mute. There was no scream of terror. Her abduction had the air of a grainy, old silent film due to the absence of color and the jerky, dreamlike movement of the beasts.

In under a minute she was out of sight, consumed by the darkness.

The events leading up to her abduction began earlier when I left my bedroom with Mr. D. in tow. Within seconds the two of us walked into an ambush. We got to the bottom step of that huge three-story circular staircase when Mr. D. stopped and began to growl; he would go no farther. I turned and looked at him, somewhat astonished, because he rarely growls. He has such a good disposition. It was unlike him.

I stared at him and asked, "What's wrong?"

From inside the adjacent parlor, big Mark said in a calm and steady voice, "Joaquin, pick up Mr. Dangerous and hold on to him."

I looked through the arches that frame the foyer, and into the parlor. When I saw—what I saw—I turned and picked up Mr. D. He was shaking. I didn't know what to do, so I began to step backward, away from the staircase and toward the front door. My movement was slow and unsure. I felt a warm wetness and realized Mr. D. had inadvertently peed on my arm. Urine trickled onto the floor. I held him closer to me as he shook. His little ears were completely flat upon his head. His eyes were large and filled with fear.

In the parlor beyond, De La Santos, Mark, and Lord Leighton were in a standoff with three wolflike beasts. Mark had a rifle and was aiming it at them. Lord Leighton had a gun in his jittery right palm, and De La Santos looked very sure of himself with a gun in each hand. Despite the bandaged arm, his arms were rigidly extended in front of him. He stood there with the swagger of an American gangster and the assurance of a Western sharpshooter.

One of the beasts moved on its back legs toward the foyer. We all watched as it stood under an arch. Its snout rose up slowly and sniffed the air; moving from side to side, it drank in the aroma of fear that saturated the environment. Then, *bam!* One of them, still in the parlor, ran directly at Leighton. Leighton, in a flash, fired off a shot—wildly—before he was knocked to the ground by the beast. De La Santos and Mark instinctively turned toward Leighton, and as they did the other two dashed, with a swishing sound, into the foyer and toward the staircase. They scaled the staircase on the tips of their feet with the quickness of snakes, hissing as they ascended to the second floor. Mark took his rifle by the barrel and swung it at the head of the beast attacking Leighton. The gun smashed against the animal's skull. As it fell away from a very frightened Leighton, De La Santos, with an absolute calmness that bordered on being matter-of-fact, put a bullet in the animal's skull.

Leighton barely had enough time to get to his feet before we heard Theodora's scream, followed by an enormous crash. De La Santos led the charge up the staircase. Mark and Leighton followed and I, having no other choice, brought up the rear, but not with D-Dog still in my arms. As I began my ascent, Mr. D. wiggled his way out of my arms and, once on the ground, ran in the opposite direction. I watched him hurry away before I raced to my bedroom to join the other three at the broken window. There we watched as Theodora was whisked away into the night. I turned away from the broken window frame and wanted to sit down and momentarily catch my breath, but remembered D-Dog.

I immediately ran downstairs to find him. Behind the kitchen door he sat, cleaning his right front paw with his tongue. He looked up at me with large, sad eyes and then went back to his paw bath. He appeared to be okay. I left him behind the door and got a glass of water before sitting down at the kitchen table. It didn't take long before he came out and sat at my feet.

I could hear the three of them out in the parlor. They appeared to be arguing. I had no desire to find out what they were arguing about because I knew we would have to come to a decision and I wouldn't like any of the options. Instead, I asked Mr. D. if he wanted some water. He didn't respond but I got it for him anyway. He looked at it and took a couple of licks, but I really don't think he was thirsty. He just drank it because I gave it to him. I picked him up and kissed him a few times. He liked that and licked me on the cheek. Looking into this face, I told him I was going into the other room and if he wanted to come, he could.

I sat him down on the floor and walked toward the doorway, looking back as I moved across the kitchen. He didn't follow me. In the hallway I continued to look back, and finally, when I got to the parlor's door stoop, I saw him stick his head into the hall apprehensively.

Leighton, Mark, and De La Santos stood around the dead beast. Suicide, or as Mark put it, *"felo de se,"* is what everyone wanted to avoid, so while it may have appeared less than honorable, we wouldn't go in search of Theodora that night. They came for her, Mark reasoned, so they wouldn't kill her right away—though her death seemed inevitable without our help.

No one was quite sure why they had taken Theodora. Mark firmly believed Don Humberto was behind it, that he wanted her for reasons better left unmentioned.

"For a bride?" I asked.

Mark looked me up and down and chuckled. "Something like that," he said.

Leighton suggested a possibility inconceivable to me. "How do we know she was taken for Don Humberto? Could she have been taken for an *unnatural* reason?"

The bewilderment on my face forced him to explain.

"Perhaps," he said, "She is not to be the bride of Don Humberto or even part of his concubine but rather the bride of another. Could her tragic fate be that she is to be united, for eternity, with a beast that we have yet to encounter?"

Mr. De La Santos said Don Humberto was unbalanced; everyone in San Felipe was aware of that fact. He said there were rumors of "experiments" taking place in Don Humberto's castle, but no one who ever spoke of such things lived long enough to prove them. He didn't foresee marriage in Don Humberto's future.

At daybreak, it was decided, we would load ourselves up with enough guns and ammunition to annihilate a small Mexican village and drive to the castle that Don Humberto used as his home; it was, of course, the house on the hill. The one I had seen from my window.

After Leighton had a "stiffener" he began to probe the dead carcass on the parlor floor. It was half man, half beast with low spikes on its back. The spikes weren't sharp but rather rounded at the tips. Its hair was sparse in places and it appeared to be missing large patches of fur. Leighton used a rifle to open the beast's mouth, and we all looked at the sharp teeth that were yellowed and black. I asked if anyone had called the police. As De La Santos aimed his revolver at the beast, cocking the hammer and releasing it without ever firing, he said in a monotone voice that they wouldn't come, what with the earthquake and its aftermath. This meant we alone would be responsible for Theodora's rescue.

I admit freely that I am a coward. I lack the courage and strength necessary to fight another man, so I don't know how I will fare in our mission tomorrow. I hope I will not embarrass myself and will have the fortitude to face the unknown with bravery. I also hope I am not liable for any mishaps that will negatively affect anyone in our group. With luck, my timidness and lack of aggression will in no way be responsible for anyone's death. My course of action is to pray and to ask our heavenly father for guidance. Mr. D. found what I needed to find. He made his way into the parlor, growling as he approached. He was leery of the dead beast on the oriental carpet but still wanted to have a sniff. He spent so much time circling the carcass; it took forever for him to work up the courage to actually get close enough to sniff it, and when he did, he quickly ran backward straight into an overstuffed ottoman.

With all but one of us sure it was dead, we dragged the animal by its back feet out of the parlor, across the large foyer, through the double front doors, and onto the veranda. Leighton said there was only one way to be sure it was dead— decapitate it. He took a large axe De La Santos had found in an outbuilding and hacked at the beast's neck. It seemed to come back briefly to our sphere after the first whack. Its eyes glowed with life, but that only made Leighton strike faster and harder with subsequent blows. It was actually quite difficult to sever the beast's head, taking at least a quarter of an hour. We left the headless body on the veranda as a warning to its associates; Leighton stood its head upright on the top step like a bizarre monstrous pumpkin. I'm not sure that was necessary.

I moved into Theodora's room for the night and we locked the door on my old bedroom. I kept the skeleton key. Everybody had a sleeping companion that evening; a .38, a .45, a rifle, or a shotgun. The gun under my pillow didn't give me too much reassurance, simply because I didn't know how to use it. That didn't bother Mr. D., though. He slept so close to my chest that night that I could hear his heartbeat.

In the morning we discovered that the headless beast on the veranda, in Mr. De La Santos's words, *"No está aquí."* No one believed it had gotten up and walked away. Leighton said it was all "sixes and sevens" because there was only one believable explanation: "others" had snuck here during the night and removed the body. It was time for our lesson.

After a bachelor breakfast, which consisted of standing over the kitchen table while eating apples and drinking coffee, Mr. De La Santos took the three of us out onto the bloody veranda and, armed with firepower, gave us shooting lessons. Upon the completion of an hour's instruction I would have to say that I'm not the best shot. Mark is a natural. He is a born killer and didn't even know it before today. Every time he hit the target he strutted around like an urban pimp with his chest pushed out.

Then he would say stuff like "Who da man?" and "I'm a badass."

He strutted up and down the veranda, gestured to his big round butt, and said, "Look at this bad ass."

While Leighton and De La Santos found him amusing, his behavior was slightly annoying for someone having difficulty, like myself. Normally, I would request that he engage in some modesty, but in this situation I was simply grateful he could hit the target. Lord Leighton and I didn't fare as well. De La Santos put some oranges and grapefruits on wooden crates as targets, but they were impossible for us to hit, so he scrounged up some old bottles from various outbuildings. The two of us had more success with the bottles, but I still wouldn't place anybody's life in the hands of Leighton or myself.

Within a half hour of the last bullet being fired, the Impala was loaded up and Mark and Leighton were already sitting in the vehicle on the passenger sides. I had put out enough food and water in the kitchen to last Mr. D. for the day. I also put some paper down on the kitchen floor just in case. D-Dog was in the house. The front door was locked and it was then that I merely suggested that, maybe, we might take some sandwiches with us.

Mark said, "Geez, Joaquin, we're not going on a frickin' picnic."

De La Santos looked at me in an unsure way and said rather hesitantly, *"Vámanos?"*

He gestured with his head toward the car.

I stood frozen.

Mark crinkled up his nose as if he had just seen something distasteful and said, "Joaquin, if you don't get in this car and come with us, you will regret it *and* be ashamed of your actions for the rest of your life. So get in, bud. We're waiting."

I didn't move.

Mark smiled one of his fake smiles and said in a sweet, saccharine voice, "Oh, and whenever I recount this story in the future I will refer to you as the Biggest Punk-Ass Wuss *ever*. So sack up!"

I crossed my arms in front of my chest and moved toward the car. De La Santos opened the door and I slid into the backseat next to Leighton. I stared at the back of Mark's head and thought Theodora might be right when she called Mark Crowden that word that I won't repeat. De La Santos jumped in and started the car.

That's when Mark turned back and said, "Anyway, the worst thing that can happen is we'll all end up dead."

He paused.

"Well, that wouldn't be the worst thing," Mark continued. "The worse thing would be if the Chupacabras tried to mate with one of us." His eyes got big and he pretended to shiver in fear. "Since I'm the prettiest one in this crackpot crew, I need to ugly myself up."

Mark looked around the car. He pointed at Leighton and said, "Quick! Switch shirts with me!"

Leighton threw his head back and howled with laughter as De La Santos floored it and the Impala peeled out; the back wheels went sideways before straightening, dust swirled into a cloud, and I covered my mouth as I coughed.

It took no time at all to get there. The front of the building looked completely different from the rear and appeared to be designed by Henry Hobart Richardson. It was a three-story Romanesque-style house. Constructed of red sandstone blocks, there were two massive turrets, one on each side. With eyelike windows in the roof, it was capped with cast-iron cresting all along the roof area. There was an enormous front door and the structure had all the elements of nineteenth-century beauty. A disquieting aspect of the house was that it appeared to be covered in moldy ivy; clinging to the ivy were cobwebs that moved. I looked at the structure as I strapped on my holster. Fortunately, I had brought along some leather tooling equipment with me to Mexico, so I was able to emboss a large cross onto the holster last night after dinner. Nothing showy; nothing "fancy schmancy," as Theodora would say. It was a very tasteful and restrained design simply to ward off any evil spirits.

Leighton wore a sidearm.

Mark and De La Santos wore holsters *and* carried shotguns.

We were going to take the direct approach, going up to the front door and knocking, but first we had to get through a massive iron gate attached to a high stone wall that surrounded the property; large crows sat on the wall and squawked at us.

They moved along the wall acting as if they were about to fly off but instead remained where they were, studying us. The iron gate contained depictions of individuals at death's door: a man was being guillotined while a hooded executioner stood beside him; a woman hung from a noose; various men were impaled on spears; a man was being stretched on a wheel; a woman was being torn apart by four horses; a hooded criminal sat in an electric chair.

Wolflike beasts ran above and below the execution depictions.

De La Santos pulled on the gate, but it was locked. His large forearm attempted to rattle it loose, but even he couldn't budge the gate free. As De La Santos and Mark tried to figure out how to scale the wall, a man from "across the void" walked up to the gate. He was on the inside but was close enough for me to watch as his eyes rolled back into their sockets, eerily revealing only the whites. His head tilted back as if his neck was broken. This gatekeeper did not appear to be looking at the gate as he opened it for us, while remaining silent. As we walked through, the man handed Leighton a small white business card. Leighton read the card, laughed, and handed it to De La Santos and Mark. They read it and handed it to me. On the card were printed the words *Death is but steps away.* I threw it on the ground and wiped my fingers on my shirt. I stared at the dirt-covered card and wished I had brought some hand sanitizer.

We walked up the cracked concrete sidewalk, but the closer we got to the house, the more the ivy moved. The three of them kept walking, but I stopped when I saw the first snake slithering vertically down the front of Don Humberto's house. How was that possible? The cobwebs that covered the ivy were spun by large, hairy spiders that dripped some sort of saliva substance from their mouths. The whole front of the house seemed to be moving in a variety of crazy, unpatterned directions—that is, until the three of them got to the first step, and then the movement stopped. An opening through the ivy allowed access to the front door, but no one walked onto the porch because something unsettling happened.

A large crow sat on a low wall that ran adjacent to the house. This wall was only about three feet high, and when the home was built there were probably beds of flowers growing on both sides. The crow sat on the wall cawing and looking at Mark, who waved at the bird with his palm flat down. He moved his hand up and down as if he were patting the head of a dog. The crow, like many humans, seemed transfixed by Mark and his weird behavior, and that's precisely why it didn't see it coming. Two large spiders jumped from the ivy onto the crow. They bit into its neck and clung to it as the crow fell from the wall. The crow screeched. It rolled around on the ground, its wings flapping as it fought and tried to get away. With each screech, more spiders jumped from the ivy and scurried over to feast on the crow. The crow continued to fight, its wings banging against the dirt as it moved in a circular motion, but its efforts became less and less vigorous until finally the crow stopped flapping its wings altogether and its body became a meal. It lay lifeless on the ground as spiders covered it and ravenously chewed on the fresh meat.

The four of us watched the scene play out. Mark turned and looked back at me.

"Joaquin, get up here," he said. "I don't want you straggling behind."

I hesitantly moved forward. But as I walked toward them, I said, "I know this is going to sound uncaring, but I recommend that we walk back down this sidewalk, get in the car, return to the Cascada, pick up Mr. D., and drive back to the United States."

They all stared at me, speechless.

I extended my hands in front of me, palms up. "Somebody has to say it. A rational suggestion has to be made by one of us."

Lord Leighton looked at me for a moment, turning over the words I had just uttered, before he said, "Are you saying you would like to leave Miss Russell here?"

I didn't respond. I was too embarrassed to actually admit that was what I was proposing.

Leighton waved away my misgivings. "Not to worry, young man. We will succeed in this endeavor and it will be a triumph against all odds. You'll see. But this is no time to squabble. Get on with it. Find your courage and join us."

He stood looking at me, defying me to disagree with him.

De La Santos smiled. He seemed to understand my fear, yet I failed to understand how he could—being the man he was.

Mark, of course, had the final world. "It may be irrational, Joaquin, but we have no choice. Sometimes in life there is only one option for a man."

I knew he was right. He's usually right. I took a deep breath and walked to them.

Mark put his arm around my shoulder and said, "I won't let anything happen to you, weasel-boy."

He smiled and gave me a big bear hug. While his words were reassuring, even I know Mark isn't a superman.

We could no longer delay our mission. As a group, we lifted our heads and looked up at the ivy-covered house in front of us; a wall of snake and spider eyes looked down upon us.

"Buck up, men," said Leighton. "No need to feel intimidated. We've all been in posher places than this." He looked at us with determination before saying, "Let's go find Miss Russell."

We ascended the stairs in a tight group. I kept looking behind us as I held on to one of Mark's back belt loops. We crossed the cement porch and Leighton put his hand on the bronze doorknob. He turned back to smile as he cautiously twisted the knob to the right. The door's mechanism clicked and my eyes were transfixed on Leighton's hand as he pushed the door open with the tips of his four fingers. A mildewy smell greeted us. The room was covered in dust; it looked abandoned.

"What an excellent room," said Leighton.

It had a gothic interior that bordered on being medieval with white cement walls, a vaulted ceiling with wood straps that followed the ceiling's structure, churchlike furnishings, and thick green-and-gold brocade curtains. We walked farther into the room with the only sound being our footsteps. Leighton didn't speak, but he motioned with his pistol to a closed set of pocket doors across the room. He tiptoed to one of them and De La Santos quietly went to the other. On each side they put their fingers into the recessed handles. Leighton looked into De La Santos's face and nodded. They each pulled their respective door back slowly. It led to another room, which didn't look nearly as nice as the first. It had large blotchy water stains on the walls and the furniture was tattered. The room was huge, with a high ceiling that had peeling paint in a variety of spots. It was also noticeably cooler than the previous room.

Very little light entered the space because the window shades were pulled down. The sides of the shades had curled and cracked and darkened due to their age. At the far end of this room was an enormous wooden door that was rounded at the top. It had to be at least ten feet tall. The wood was gray and covered in moisture; drips of water made their way down the grooves in the door and puddled on the floor. It had an elaborate escutcheon and rusted hardware straps forged of wrought iron. My eyes were drawn to all of it, and I knew what we were looking for was beyond the dripping door.

Leighton, pistol in hand, walked up to it and pulled it open just wide enough for the barrel of his gun to fit through. He looked back at us and smiled. Then he flung it open with a wide sweeping arm gesture. The door squeaked while it moved slowly open to a stop. His gesture and all its bravado didn't seem very wise, but the rest of us joined him at the doorway. On the other side was a long, high, dark, narrow hallway. It appeared wet and was cold enough that I could see my breath though I was standing a few yards away. Along both sides of the hallway were tall marble Doric columns; they were spaced out approximately every ten feet, in pairs.

As if in slow motion, Leighton turned from looking down the long hallway to the three of us. He said in a calm and whispery voice, "Narrow is the road that leads to life and few find it."

I looked at him and said, "You're quoting scripture?"

"Matthew 7:14."

Mark looked at Leighton and said, "We're not in that much trouble, are we?"

With eyes almost manic with excitement, Leighton said, "Yes, Mr. Crowden, we are."

Lord Leighton seemed thrilled that we were on the

threshold of the unknown, and I did not understand why. The farther we progressed into this house, the less chance we had of ever getting out. We seal our doom when we move forward.

I wanted to turn back and leave, but was brought back to our pressing duty when Leighton said, "Don't you understand, gentlemen?"

He looked for some acknowledgment from us. We gave him none. He reached across the open doorway and pulled back an imaginary curtain. He shuffled his feet like a tap dancer and then put his hands in front of his eyes and nose, covering them completely, leaving only his mouth visible.

I watched his lips move as he said, "We are in the lair of the Chupacabras."

Leighton bowed at the waist and said, "Gentlemen first."

Mark took a step, but I held him back by his belt loop.

I peeked around Mark's body and said, "After you."

Leighton stood up, removed his hands from his face, and shook his head slightly, as if to get the Chupacabras out of his head before he stood rigidly erect. Very formally, he said, "Of course. Bravery is a characteristic the English have always held in high esteem what with Churchill, Cromwell, Nelson, and their lot."

I pulled out my flashlight nervously and turned it on. My amigos watched as I extended my arm and pointed down the hallway. Our eyes followed the light's beam as it explored the darkness we were about to enter. Leighton took a deep breath and held it in for about ten seconds. I did not know what he would do next. Despite only being able to see Lord Leighton's stocky frame from behind, and with a mountain of Mark partially blocking my view, it was still evident he had to force himself to proceed. His hesitancy was the clue. He needed to regain his footing on his own. He righted himself, and when he did, he didn't look back for reassuring support or to make any pro-British statements about war and valor, he simply stepped away from us unassumingly. I admired him at that moment and used his comportment as an example for myself as we continued our search for Theodora.

The glow of my flashlight followed him. I kept the flashlight's beam focused near the center of his back. Since I still held on to Mark's belt loop, he and I moved as one. Mr. De La Santos brought up the rear.

Leighton tapped on one of the columns and said, "These *are* marble."

His voice echoed off the walls. I looked up and noticed that there was barely any ceiling left. There had been a barrel ceiling, but most of the plaster had fallen away and what remained was lathe interspersed with large holes. Above it, beyond the immediate darkness, I could see small rays of sunlight penetrating through the damaged roof.

In no time at all Leighton had gotten much farther ahead of us. He was at the seventh or eighth set of columns while we had only reached the third set when it happened.

Mark had just said, in an annoyed voice, "Slow down. What's your hurry?"

I raised the flashlight higher so its beam was elevated six or seven feet above the floor, for Leighton appeared to be levitating, but he wasn't—yet he *was* being lifted off the ground. One of the creatures was perched on a column and it was holding Leighton in the air by his head. The creature's entire palm covered the top of Leighton's skull; its claws dug into his sculp. Blood ran down Leighton's face. He was suspended almost precisely in the center of the hallway, for the creature had risen on its back legs and had its right front arm extended completely out and away from its body. Leighton's arms flailed about. It appeared as if he was trying to get to his gun but his motor skills were impaired due to his situation.

He said in a monotone voice, "Gentlemen, please do something."

De La Santos lifted up his shotgun and cocked the trigger, but it was already too late.

On the opposite column another creature rose up with an axe in hand, and just as I heard a shot from De la Santos's gun, the axe's blade hit Leighton in the throat. His body seemed to sag from its own weight as it pulled away from the head. A large gash in his throat emitted an avalanche of blood.

Leighton said, "Fiddle-faddle," in a garbled, blood-soaked voice as blood spurted out of his mouth.

De La Santos fired again just as Leighton's body ripped away from his head and landed on the ground with a muffled thud. The creature then threw Leighton's head against the wall in an unsanctified manner. With their mission accomplished, the creatures took a moment to screech triumphantly upon their pedestals, turning in different directions so all could hear. After they finished, they scurried upward and climbed into the ravaged ceiling, vanishing into the darkness.

Mark broke my grip on his belt loop as he ran to Leighton's body.

He yelled out in the darkness, "Joaquin, bring that flashlight up here."

I directed the flashlight's glow upon Leighton's body.

Mark was kneeling next to Leighton when I spoke. "Can you carry his body?"

Mark made the sign of the cross and then looked up at me. He nodded.

I uttered a sentence I could have never imagined, saying, "I'll carry his head."

De La Santos seemed confused. He had tilted his head down at an angle and squinted his eyes.

Mark looked at De La Santos and said, "We have to take his body. That's one of the tenets of the Odd Fellows. We bury the dead."

I was taking off my shirt as I said with as much authority as I could muster, "Mark's not going to be able to shoot on our way out of here."

I pointed at De La Santos.

"You have to make sure he gets out of here safely. Do you understand?"

I was embarrassed that my voice raised a teeny bit and I seemed breathless as I spoke. De La Santos smiled and gave me a thumbs-up. He took a stick of gum out of his pocket, unwrapped it, and put it in his mouth right before he helped Mark lift Leighton's body up and onto Mark's shoulder. Leighton's legs were against Mark's chest and Mark clasped his arms over them. Leighton's upper body hung down Mark's back; blood continued to drip from the open neck cavity.

As soon as Mark felt secure with Leighton's placement he turned to me and said, "Okay, Joaquin, get his head."

I set my shirt down on the ground and without any hesitation picked up Leighton's head and placed it on the open shirt. As I looked at his face a bubble of saliva formed on his lips; it wiggled back and forth in an effort to escape, did so, and began its journey. I watched as it took its time to drift up toward the light above—beyond the vast darkness we found ourselves in. When I couldn't see it anymore, I bowed my head, crossed myself with blessed reverence, and said under my breath, *May God have mercy on his soul.* I looked at his face and observed how damaged and bloody it was. Their attack on him was beyond vicious. It was revenge.

I made a vow to Lord Leighton right there: "I promise you will receive a proper Christian burial."

With that said, I hurried back to my duty, wrapped my shirt around his head, and stood up. I held it in the crook of my left arm as I pulled my gun out of its holster and gave Mark and De La Santos a nod that said, "I'm ready."

De La Santos said, *"Vámanos."*

We were off. He took the lead, Mark and the body in the middle, and I brought up the rear. I backed out of the hallway with my gun ready and cocked. We had no trouble traversing the tattered, water-stained room. While De La Santos seemed unfazed by what had happened, the events had certainly affected Mark and me. We both moved in circles through the room, unsure of what was behind us and afraid of what was ahead. As we crossed into Leighton's "excellent room," I felt more confident that we might make it back to Mr. D.

De La Santos ran to the front door, but he appeared to run in a telescopic fashion. He would run and then zoom to a stop. He would run again and then stop again. Run more and stop. It was as if his movement was freezing. I was seeing double, triple, and quadruple images of him. They moved in and out and then back together again like an accordion. It was not natural and it did not seem to be taking place in real time, but it was.

I chalked up my false vision to the shock I was surely experiencing. Once at the door, De La Santos discovered an obstacle that prevented us from leaving. Not only was the door locked, but a metal grate had been lowered on the inside.

De La Santos looked around the room and then at Mark and me before he said, "We're going out the window, *jefe.*"

Mark, slightly winded, said, "Tell me it's a window not covered in spiders and snakes."

"That's the only kind we got here, Señor Crowden."

De La Santos went to the windows and started to rip down the green-and-gold brocade curtains. The curtain hardware made a loud noise as it fell to the floor, clanking like heavy chains. Mark and I watched him. Mark's head was slightly tilted down and at an angle; the weight of Leighton's body was starting to take a toll.

I asked Mark if he wanted to put the body down and he responded by shaking his head vigorously and saying in a booming voice, "Fe fi fo fum. I've got the strength of a giant! A *giant*, I tell you."

I wasn't sure how to respond.

Mark looked around the room in search of a more appreciative audience and then said "harrumph," after which he blew a long stream of air out of his mouth, and I watched the moist hair on his forehead move slightly. He wearily said, "Somebody's going to have to rub salve on my back tonight."

I nodded even though he hadn't asked if I would do it or not. I simply wanted to be encouraging since a drizzly, gray cloud had momentarily appeared over his head. He looked sad standing there, shouldering the dead weight.

We both turned our attention to Mr. De La Santos as he walked up to us.

"We'll need these." He handed me one of the brocade curtains. "Fold it over twice," he said. "Put it over your head and cover as much of your body as you can."

He looked me in the eyes. *"Tú vas primero."*

I blinked my eyes like a catfish just pulled from the Mississippi. Then I gulped.

"Once you get outside," he continued, "take off running, *mijo*. Don't stop till you get to the gate."

I nodded.

"Throw off the curtain whenever you think it's safe."

"I'll go second. I'll help Señor Crowden get out with the body."

I put Leighton's head down on the couch, put the curtain over my head, and covered most of my body. The only visible parts of me were my feet, the bottom of my pants, and my eyes. I was one big walking brocade curtain.

Mark looked at me and said, "You look like the Virgin Mary but a Mexican version, so I guess that would make you the Virgin de Guadalupe."

He tried to sound Latino when he said that. I mumbled something under the curtain that I won't repeat.

Mark responded by saying, "What? Are you trying to say something, precious?"

I shook my head. Mark turned his head and yelled over his shoulder, "Hey, De La Santos, this dead body's gettin' heavy. Can we hurry it up?"

The giant was tired.

De La Santos ran over and put a curtain over Mark, then raced up to the front window, turned to us, and said, "Ready?"

He pulled a curtain over his shoulders and tied the ends of it together at his waist, rather loosely, and then took the butt of his shotgun and began to break the window's glass. His action made a terrific amount of noise. Over and over he shoved the shotgun's butt through the glass. It tinkled onto the porch.

De La Santos looked at me with an agitated look and yelled, *"Listo!"*

I hurried to the window, looked out, and gasped in what only could be termed as fear before I took a deep breath. I wasn't going underwater, but I had a feeling I would be hyperventilating soon. The entire porch was covered in spiders.

Snakes were slithering amongst them, but it was the spiders that made the impression by scurrying everywhere like murderous mini-machines. I lifted the curtain higher and looked to De La Santos for encouragement. He didn't say a word. He lifted his eyebrows and tilted his head toward the window. For some reason that was not what I expected. I smiled sheepishly, climbed up on the windowsill, took a deep breath, and jumped. My feet could feel the spiders as they imploded and squirted underneath my shoes. The whole swarm of them started to screech as I took off running, gun in one hand and Leighton's head clutched to my chest with the other. I felt squirting under my feet as I killed more and more. I was running faster than I've ever run and felt spiders landing on me, so I moved my body jerkily under the curtain. I envisioned myself at the gate and saw myself running toward it. The brocade curtain flew about me; I appeared to be a colorful dead spirit as spiders jumped on me, bounced off me, and clung to the curtain.

Nearly at the gate I flung the curtain off so that it flew high into the air. It sailed aloft covered in spiders, swirling away from me into the sky. I watched as it flew off like a magic carpet. The spiders clung to it. I put my gun in its holster and brushed off my hair and shoulders. I stood and watched as Mark and De La Santos ran toward me. I must have gotten the worst of it. By going first I had scattered them and inadvertently made their escape easier. As they reached me and tossed their brocade protection away, one final task awaited us as Odd Fellows.

VIII.
Mark Crowden's Blog: Bury the Dead

Joaquin looked down at me and said, "I think it's the most perfect grave ever dug."

I stood in a six-foot-deep grave with a shovel. Sweat dripped down the sides of my face and ran down my chest and back, too.

I used the back of my hand to wipe the sweat off my face and said, "Weren't you going to bring me *una cerveza?*"

Joaquin held his index finger up in the air to indicate he needed a minute, rushed over to the front porch, pulled a beer out of a bucket of ice, hurried back to the graveside, and handed it to me.

I unscrewed the top and took a long drink. *"Ah, muy bueno."*

I looked Joaquin over and searched for the other thing he knew he should have brought me.

"Did you bring me a paper towel?"

Joaquin didn't say anything. I watched as his eyes moved back and forth like the eyes in one of those novelty cat clocks. He squeezed his lips together before he pulled a folded paper towel out of his pocket. He had folded it over so many times that it was a two-inch square. He held it out for me to take, but it was practically hidden between his thumb and index finger.

I said in mock shock, "That's it?"

The only feedback I received from him was a slight head nod.

I took it from him with *my* index finger and thumb. My three other fingers fanned out like a…a…a fan. I turned my hand back and forth so I could see the back of my hand and then the palm, the back of my hand and then the palm; all the while I squeezed the minutely folded paper towel.

"It's so tiny," I said.

Joaquin just looked at me like I was flipping stupid. I took the little square and without unfolding it dabbed my forehead and then my nose daintily.

Joaquin mutely stared at me for a moment before he said, "You look like Marie Antoinette when you do that."

I faked some outrage and said, "I am so offended by that comment." My voice raised dramatically when I said the word *offended*.

Joaquin, of course, in his typical fashion did not respond.

"Well, I don't know if I take very kindly to that attitude, origami-boy."

I carefully unfolded the paper towel, which I discovered he had folded over five times. I looked at all the folded creases.

"It should still work," I said in an effort to make things right even though they hadn't gone too wrong.

I took the paper towel and placed it over my face so it covered practically all of it. It stuck rather well. Sweat can be an adhesive! I proceeded to walk around inside the grave with the paper towel attached to my face.

I held my hands out in front of myself and said, "Look at me. Look at me. I can't see. I can't see. Oh my God. I be blind."

In reality I could see a hazy Joaquin through the paper towel's fibers.

He stared at me and said, "You have a paper towel stuck to your face, you nutso."

"Nutso?"

With my arms stuck out I stopped and shook my whole body. I probably looked like I had been electrocuted by three whole volts of limp electricity. I stopped shaking and very delicately and slowly pulled the paper towel off my face.

"Oh, that's what it is."

Joaquin tried to suppress a smile but I could still see it no matter how much he tried. He turned his attention away from me, which was rude, and to the mound of dirt next to the grave.

"So when do you want to bury him?" he asked.

I walked up to the side of the grave and put my arms down flat on the edge, still holding the bottle; it was the type of stance someone would take while standing at the edge of a pool. It's a pose I've done many a time, and it gives me a virile look that can't escape anyone's eyes. I know that sounds conceited, but in my defense, it is *so* true.

"Well, how about if I take a shower, clean up, and since

this is an end-of-life ceremony, why don't we bury him at twilight?"

Joaquin nodded. "Do you want help getting out?"

I shook my head, took off my sombrero, and hoisted myself out of the grave. Regrettably, this act was not performed in the most graceful manner; I suspect I looked like a big, fat walrus as I pulled myself out onto my belly and then rolled over. I made walrus noises as I rolled around on my back, raised my arms away from my body, and clapped my hands like I had flippers. Joaquin looked at me in silence. I got up and brushed myself off. Sometimes my charm even evades Joaquin.

As we walked toward the house together I said, "If I did this for a living I could lose some weight."

Joaquin, who has always been extremely truthful and honest, said, "You look fine the way you are."

"Yes," I said. "If I ever need a character witness in court I'm taking you with me since you would be under oath and would be required, by law, to tell the truth."

I detected a very subtle snort from Joaquin. It was almost inaudible.

I continued, "Once when Frank Lloyd Wright was on the witness stand, a lawyer asked him about himself and Wright said something to the effect of 'I'm the greatest architect in the world.' The lawyer looked at him, rather astonished, and Wright responded, 'Well, I'm under oath, so I *must* tell the truth.'"

"You could sit on the witness stand and when they asked you about me you could say, let's see, uh, I don't want to put words in your mouth, but it could be something like, 'Mark Crowden is the finest specimen of male virility the world has ever known.'"

Joaquin started to laugh, which was really inappropriate but I overlooked it as I wanted him to get his line down right.

"Okay, say it after me, 'Mark Crowden is...'"

Through some giggles, which almost made it appear as if he was hesitant to say it, Joaquin began, "Mark Crowden is..."

I continued, "The finest specimen of male virility the world has ever known."

Joaquin could barely contain his laughter at this point and he was almost completely incomprehensible as he said, "The finest specimen of male virility the world has ever known."

He wasn't very convincing.

After I took a swig of beer, I pointed at him with my finger, which I wished was a stun gun, and said, "You're not going to be believable on the witness stand if you're laughing when you say it."

Joaquin looked at me with a blank face and tried to suppress a snorting noise. He didn't do that too well, either. He's not going to be a very good defense witness in my imaginary trial—which could be a matter of life and death—if he can't support me on the witness stand in my hour of need.

We had reached the porch, so I let him off the hook with "We'll practice more *mañana*."

I think I saw him roll his eyes as he looked down at the porch, but I'm not sure. I need to have a talk with that little weasel-boy.

❖

Joaquin had hand-sewn Leighton's body into a white sheet. He said it took him no time at all; it was a simple cross-stitch sewn twice over itself. He sewed the head into an oversized white pillowcase. "What else could I do?" he asked. If he had sewn the head and body into the same body bag, the head would have rolled around, which, according to Joaquin, would have been tantamount to sacrilege.

De La Santos and I carried the body to the grave. Joaquin carried the head. We set both parts down on the ground adjacent to the grave and then De La Santos went back to the porch and brought a ladder he had found in the basement. It was dusk when we finally began; it was an "end of the day" ceremony, in Joaquin's words. I jumped down into the grave and De La Santos lowered Leighton's body to me. I placed him flat on his back in the center of the grave. When I looked up, Joaquin was handing me the head. I placed it above the body where it should have been. De La Santos then lowered the ladder into the grave at the foot end and I climbed out. We removed the ladder.

I looked at Joaquin, nodded, and said, "You begin."

Joaquin made the sign of the cross and De La Santos and I followed suit.

Joaquin spoke. "Our father who art in heaven, hallowed be thy name. Thy kingdom come, thy will be done, on earth as it is in heaven. Give us this day our daily bread, and forgive us our trespasses as we forgive those who trespass against us, and lead us not into temptation, but deliver us from evil. Amen."

We all made the sign of the cross, then De La Santos walked to the porch and brought back three glasses and a bottle of wine. He gave each of us a glass and tried to pour an equal amount of wine into each.

We lifted our glasses and I said, "Lord Leighton, while our time on earth together was brief, we hope your journey to heaven is an exciting adventure. We have faith you will find friendship, love, and truth in heaven with Jesus Christ our savior. Amen."

We clinked our glasses together and drank to our departed amigo.

No one uttered a word for the longest time; there wasn't a sound anywhere. It was as if each and every sound had vanished from the earth.

We simply drank our wine until I finally said, "I'll start."

I walked over to the mound of dirt, picked up the shovel, and lifted a load of dirt. I tossed it gently upon Leighton and we watched as the dirt splattered upon his body. As I tossed more and more shovels of dirt upon him, I thought about how little I knew about Leighton.

It all happened so fast. He didn't even have time to think about all his yesterdays. "Narrow is the road that leads to life, and few find it." How rare is it to say the right thing at the right time? In that horrific unraveling of events, Leighton had made a pretty prophetic statement, but frickin' fiddle-dee-dee, it ended up being *my* day of deliverance. If Joaquin hadn't held me back; if I had gone first instead of Leighton, I would have been the object of the attack.

I'm not sure if I should mention it, and if I do, what could I possibly say that could keep me out from under a cloud of obligation? Maybe it's best if I opt for silence and it simply remains our trusted secret, known between the two of us as an unspoken incident that ties us together in the way that unspoken words often bind people together stronger than any glue.

❖

Earlier in the day, I walked past Joaquin's room as he was sewing Leighton's body into the three-hundred-count body bag. It was a strange sight because the head lay upon an open towel—on a pillow—in all its decapitated craziness. Sitting on his bed, Joaquin worked on encasing the corpse beside him. All the while he wore his MP3 player, which is probably why he didn't look up as I stood and peeked at him from the hallway. He sang along to a song quietly and his voice really wasn't audible; I couldn't decipher what the song was. Mr. D. walked around on the bed and sniffed both body and head; he, too, was so engrossed in his endeavor that he failed to notice me. I walked to my room, picked up my camera, and returned and focused my lens on the three of them. I clicked the shutter. I clicked the shutter again and Joaquin looked up.

He spoke very loudly due to the headphones. "Why don't you take Mr. D. with you and go find Mr. De La Santos?"

"Why?" I asked.

Joaquin went back to his sewing as he said, "I've been sitting here wondering about his Christian name. Why don't you track him down and ask him?" Joaquin looked up and bit the thread in half with his teeth.

"I know what it is," I said.

"What is it?" Joaquin asked as he removed his headphones.

"I'll give you a clue." I held my index finger to my lips and looked up. "Think of a celebrated cat," I said.

I raised my arm up to my mouth and chewed around my wrist as if I had fleas before I licked the hair on my arm like *un gato guapo.*

"Garfield?"

I stopped licking. I looked at Joaquin blank-faced with the exception of the tip of my tongue sticking out of my mouth poised above my wrist.

"Bucky?"

Still, I gave him no response. My muteness was unnatural and peculiar.

"My Kitty?"

I wiped my wrist and arm on my shirt and lowered my head forward to stare at him. "Are you tryin' to sandbag me with second-rate cat names? My Kitty De La Santos? Get serious, mortician boy."

Recognition crossed Joaquin's face in the way that happiness often does when the truth becomes clear.

"His name is *Felix De La Santos*," said Joaquin.

"You are correct, my little casket maker."

"When did he tell you?"

I grabbed imaginary lapels and stood with the pompousness of a man from the mid-nineteenth century. I said, "Before we went into Don Humberto's house. While we were trying to figure out how to scale the wall I said, hey, we might end up dead, so, just in case, what's your name?"

"What did he say to that?"

"He laughed. Not à la Pagliacci, but it was a laugh all the same."

❖

Felix De La Santos walked up to me, took the shovel from my hand, and began to shovel. Later Joaquin did the same for Felix. While Joaquin was on shovel duty I went inside and let Mr. D. out. He raced to the graveside, curious about what was going on, and raced around making quick stops and then furiously taking off again; he sniffed everything and everybody. When he finally calmed down, Felix picked him up, petted him on the head, and kissed him on the belly, which he always likes. He squirmed in Mr. De La Santos's arms and licked his cheek in a slow and deliberate fashion. It was dark when we finally finished. Felix went and retrieved a rusted old lantern that emitted a creaky glow and a cross he had assembled that afternoon out of distressed fence posts. He planted the cross in the place of honor, and the four of us stood in the darkness, with the only light coming from the old lantern Felix held.

Without saying a word, Mr. De La Santos left. He sat the lantern down next to the grave and walked back to the house. I didn't say anything to Joaquin when I left, but when I got to the porch I turned for a backward glance. I could see very clearly the silhouette of the cross and the row of three in profile: the glowing lantern, Mr. D. sitting on his back legs, and Joaquin kneeling with his hands clasped together in prayer. He prays so much. I shook my head. He never does anything wicked. Unlike me, he knows nothing about the wages of sin. Could he be the real oddity or could it be possible that people pray that often? What could he possibly get out of it?

The next day we decided to go to the authorities. We had no choice, and all of this had to be thrust upon professionals. When we had originally arrived back at Cascada with the dead body, we'd laid Leighton's body parts out on the porch almost precisely where the previous decapitation victim had lain. It was there I took photographs of Lord Leighton, both body and head from various angles. We would need them to show to the authorities. It was our evidence to prove the reality of the unfolding proceedings to skeptics who would doubt both our words and motives.

We arrived at the police station and a man at the front desk directed us down a dark hallway to an officer he said would help us. He was wrong. The police sergeant was overweight. His shirt was covered in perspiration; under the arms, down the back, around the collar. His top shirt buttons were unbuttoned and his dirty, wrinkled, frayed undershirt was visible. I understood his perspiration dilemma; I, too, am a victim of the overactive pore. We who suffer from this curse should not be the subject of ridicule and disgust but rather pity and empathy.

What I couldn't understand was his attitude.

In a dismissive voice that spat out each word's syllables he said, "*There ain't no Chup-a-cab-ras!* Don't waste my time, gringos."

Felix said something in Spanish and the sergeant responded by picking up a magazine and throwing it across the room.

He got right up next to Felix, in his face, and said *very* loudly, "What are you doing with these wed-dos? What are you getting out of this?"

He used his index finger to tap his right temple. "I don't get it," he said. "You come here and ask me to help you and offer me *nothing* in return?" He continued spitting out words: "*How* can you be so inconsiderate? *How* can you show me so little respect?"

Awkwardly, I asked in a hesitant voice, "How much do you want?"

"How many doll-ors you got, señor?"

I didn't look up. I rustled through my wallet and spitballed. "I really don't have much with me." I rifled in my wallet a little more. "I have forty American dollars."

I finally looked up. I pulled two Andrew Jacksons from my wallet and held them in my right hand, out flat, like I was holding a cigarette between my index and middle fingers.

The sergeant walked up to me and ripped the money from my hand. He looked at the money with contempt. "For forty doll-ors I for-get I see the photographs of your dead friend," he said. He folded the twenty-dollar bills in half and put them in his shirt pocket. He looked at Felix and back to me.

He turned back to Felix and said, "Get out. I would not bother Don Humberto with these lies."

I looked at Felix.

He nodded and said, *"Vámanos."*

We quickly exited the police station, and once outside, Felix just as quickly raised his index finger to his lips to silence us. We walked a good thirty feet away from the buildings before he said in a hushed tone, "Don Humberto. He's no fool. *Este hombre* is giving them money, for protection. *La policía* will not help us."

Joaquin exclaimed, "The police won't help us? Why not? Don't they realize we need their help?"

Joaquin was starting to get that manic tone he gets when he's overexcited.

I very calmly turned to Joaquin and said, "Joaquin." My eyes widened and my voice rose at the end of his name. I say his name in this manner whenever I want him to calm down. It's our unspoken code for *you're getting on Markie's nerves and Markie doesn't like that.*

Joaquin quickly shut up.

I turned my attention back to Felix and asked, "Is there an American embassy in San Felipe?"

Felix shook his head and said, "There's an Americano named Hector Vance who might be able to help. Let's go see him."

Hector Vance lived in a structure that appeared to have been built in the '30s or '40s. It was a two-story house with an exterior of green stucco and an art deco flair. A black wrought-iron fence in a streamlined design surrounded the property. Hector was waiting for us outside—on his side of the fence. He did not open the gate. Instead, he watched us silently as we drove up, excised ourselves from the Impala, and walked to him.

Before any of us could speak, he said, "I cannot help you. I can only give you advice. Go back to America. What has happened to your friends is unfortunate, but you cannot help them now."

Felix began to speak. *"Hablamos..."*

Hector raised his hand to stop Felix from continuing. He shook his head and said, "I have nothing else to say."

I didn't know who this mook was, but I wasn't letting him off that easy. I blurted out, "We *need* your assistance."

Hector began to turn around as he said, "I cannot help you."

Then that ingenious little Joaquin spoke up. In a matter-of-fact, casual, "oh, by the way" way he asked, "Do you have some water for *mi perro*? He's thirsty."

Hector stopped. With his back to us he stood motionless and slowly turned around to look.

Mr. D. stood panting. His mouth was open and his tongue stuck out. His cape had a thin layer of dust upon it. Hector looked down at D-Dog, who blinked his eyes and made a pathetic little noise. It was as if he didn't even have the energy to whimper. That dog knew what he was doing. Hector's face revealed that he could not say no to the little dog in the cape, and he relented.

With a smile on his face he opened the gate and said, *"Vente.* Come in."

We filed through the gate and into his home. It was

cool inside, but the exterior belied the interior. It was not a tribute to the 1925 Exposition des arts décoratifs but rather the American arts and crafts movement of the early twentieth century. Mr. Vance went into the kitchen and I could hear water running. Mr. D. walked around the room using his nose like the nozzle of a vacuum cleaner, sniffing everything in his path and taking notes of all the smells. Hector returned with a silver tray of drinks, which he cordially dispensed. It was only lemonade, but his hospitality, after the police sergeant, was more refreshing than any drink he could have served. He was just about to sit down when he remembered the water for Mr. D. He walked back to the kitchen and returned with a shallow bowl of water, which he put down on the floor. Mr. Dangerous quickly lapped some up but stopped when a tiny Chihuahua appeared in the doorway. She immediately grabbed Mr. D.'s attention. He trotted over to the Chihuahua and sniffed her more than the leather ottoman or the dirt in the potted palm. Hector laughed, picked up the Chihuahua, and sat down on an overstuffed coach with the tiny dog on his lap.

He held her up to his face and said, "Chiquita doesn't get many callers."

He patted the sofa cushion beside himself and welcomed Mr. D. to sit on the coach. D-Dog jumped up and sat down facing Joaquin, but he looked at Chiquita out of the corners of his eyes. He was a sly one, that dog. While Hector's efforts to convince us not to return to Don Humberto's home were unsuccessful, as he spoke I noticed how amorous and playful Chiquita was. She chewed on D-Dog's tail, climbed on him, and generally acted like a little tramp. What kind of dog did Hector Vance own? Personally, I think she was a little too fast for Mr. D., but he seemed to take her advances in stride and simply lay on the couch, belly side down, with his front arms straight out; he was unresponsive as she climbed upon him and flirted like some sort of Chihuahua Jezebel.

While Hector Vance could not convince us to return to America, he was able to convince us to do one thing: to drive to 456 Orlando Street and visit Countess Pozianski. She was a Latina who married a man from Poland and now saw herself as a Polish countess. Evidently there was no basis for her leap to countess, but since her husband died, according to Hector, she had created a life for herself as a countess who offers amulets for a price and creates *pociónes* for the living. It was the *pociónes* we were after. Vance said Pozianski created a concoction that kept an individual's mind clear even under the most extreme situations.

Countess Pozianski opened the door, made the sign of the cross, and said, *"Adelante."*

She was a short woman in her sixties, around four-eleven, and dressed rather flouncy in neon yellow spandex slacks that appeared to be on the verge of splitting. She wore a blouse with a collar that was both lacy and flowery. Oh, and the lady loved the makeup; thick black eyeliner with tweezed eyebrows, black lipstick, and a white powder base.

She had to recognize that makeup could not hide her age, but she looked like she had about forty years' worth upon her face.

Her home was a cluttered shack of beauty that had experienced some earthquake damage. Ceiling plaster on one end of the room had fallen loose, and cracks weaved throughout the ceiling and walls. Amongst the wreckage were lighted candles, saint statues, and stuffed animals, with an upright bear and a large owl as standouts. Sitting on opposite sides of the main room were two marble statues on walnut pedestals. Both were of women; one was a representation of Beauty and the other was a representation of Truth. A round table with a Mexican serape as a tablecloth stood in the middle of the room with four mismatched chairs surrounding it.

She motioned for us to sit. She sat on one side of the table and the four of us sat tightly together on the other side. She lit all these candles on the table in front of us, along with incense. She spoke in a hurried, clipped, hushed manner. Mr. D. and I could barely keep up. What she said in Spanish is followed by what she really said in parentheses:

"Ustedes no sobrevivirán si ustedes vayan." (Don't go. You will not survive if you go.)

Joaquin half turned to D-Dog and me and said, "Don't go."

"Los que van no vuelven." (People don't come back.)

Without looking at us and out of the corner of his mouth Joaquin said, "Something about people not coming back."

"Ustedes experimentarán una muerte terrible." (You'll experience a terrible death.)

"We'll end up dead," Joaquin said.

"Mirarán a sus amigos morir antes sus ojos." (You'll watch your friends die in front of your eyes.)

"More death talk," Joaquin said.

"Su perro pequeño acabará por muerto también." (Your little dog will end up dead too.)

Joaquin translated that as "Mr. D. is the smartest dog ever."

"No le puedo advertir bastante." (I cannot warn you enough.)

"More warnings!" said Joaquin.

"Nadie encontrará sus cuerpos. Su sangre correrá por las puertas del infierno por la eternidad. Serán un banquete

para el Chupacabras." (No one will ever find your bodies. Your blood will run through the Gates of Hell for eternity. You will be a feast for the Chupacabras.)

Joaquin looked at D-Dog and me and said, "We won't have to pay for a funeral."

Felix bolted up and as he did, his chair fell backward upon the floor with a muffled bang.

"Vámanos," he said firmly.

She looked at Felix and stopped talking. She made the sign of the cross, rose, and went to a cabinet directly behind her. She opened it up and took out four small bags on strings. The strings were tied in loops that were big enough to fit over a head. She pushed them across the table toward us.

"Tómelos. No hay costo."

"They're free," said Joaquin.

"Pónganlos."

Joaquin indicated that we should take one. We each grabbed one and put it around our neck. Joaquin put the last one on Mr. D.

"Llévenlos siempre. Luchan el poder del Chupacabras." (Wear them always. They fight the Chupacabras's power.)

Joaquin looked at Mr. D. and me and said, "They'll help zap the Chupacabras's power."

"Huélanlos si ustedes se sienten mareos o si se sienten como si estuvieran alucinando." (Smell them if you feel light-headed or if you feel as if you're hallucinating.)

She squeezed her five fingers together on her right hand and placed them under her nose as if to demonstrate what we should do. We all sniffed the bags. Let me tell you, it didn't smell like lilacs. It had a medicinal smell. We all made strange faces with wonky eyes. I let Mr. D. sniff his. He liked it.

I took $100 out of my wallet and gave it to the countess.

"Gracias," she said.

She extended her arm toward the door, which was our clue.

As we exited I turned back.

She looked at me momentarily, closed her eyes, and lowered her head.

"Vaya con Dios."

We drove back to Cascada sniffing the bags around our necks. It had a bitter smell that opened up my nasal passages and made my eyes watery and blinky. It had to contain some menthol ingredient. It certainly made me shake my head after I sniffed it. When we arrived back at the house, the first thing Joaquin did was go up to his bedroom, take down his Odd Fellows wall hanging, and return to the large parlor with it. Felix and I sat in opposite chairs with D-Dog sprawled across Felix's lap.

Joaquin announced, "I'm wearing this from now on. I want you to pin it on me."

I squinted my eyes and said in my most goofball voice, "What?"

Joaquin repeated, "I'm wearing this from now on. I want you to use these safety pins"—he held them up, two in each hand—"and pin it on me."

"Uh," I said, "little Joaquin, are you trying to make a new fashion statement?"

Joaquin looked at me with a slightly perturbed look on his face, which was certainly unusual for him. "Would you just do it?"

I stood in front of him and asked, "How do you want to do it?"

Joaquin stood thinking for a minute. His eyes moved till he came to a decision. "Okay, I want to put the center part across the back of my waist. Bring the ends forward and cross them over my chest in an *X*. Each end goes over one of my shoulders, and then you can pin the ends to the center part across the back of my waist."

He looked up at me and nodded. "Okay?"

I pinned Joaquin up, mumbling how I felt like one of the mice in Cinderella, and stepped back.

"How do I look?" he asked.

I stood appraising him. He kind of looked like a taquito or tamale, all wrapped up like that.

"Uh, I would say...what's the right word? Oh, yeah, I know what it is. The right word would be, uh, odd. You look odd."

Felix got up and pushed past me. *"Bueno,"* he said. *"Muy bueno."*

I moved my head from side to side and looked up at the ceiling before saying, "Well, where are you going to put your gun and holster?"

I could tell Joaquin was on the verge of a silent, huffy fit. He looked at me, unsure.

"Oh, let's not have a spat," I said. "Let's be peachy."

Whatever emotion was boiling up inside Joaquin, he suppressed. He looked at me in a calculating manner as he felt along the seam of his crisscross of symbols. I watched as he felt his waistband beneath the Odd Fellows' drapery. He paused—thinking, thinking, thinking.

"I'll wear it under."

"Good," I said. I stood and looked at Joaquin.

"What?" he asked.

"With all those symbols plastered across your body, I was wondering, are you trying to scare the Chupacabras or just confuse him?"

That was the last thing I said before this big, fluffy pillow hit me in the head.

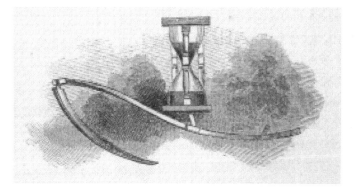

IX.

JOAQUIN MORENO'S JOURNAL: MAN'S BEST FRIEND

My best friend's silhouette was illuminated by the moonlight that found its way into our dark room. Mr. D. was standing up on the bed. His front legs were on one side of my legs and his back legs were on the other side of them. He appeared to be listening.

"What is it?" I whispered. "Do you hear something?"

He didn't respond and continued to listen. I reached out and poked him in the side with my finger. His tail wagged as he came to me and licked me on the side of the face. I poked him again and he licked me again. After he lay down beside me we must have fallen back to sleep.

I don't know how much time elapsed between that and the knock on the door, but it was dawn when I heard the knock and Mark say, "Get up and get dressed. Come downstairs and bring Mr. D."

There was a pause.

Then Mark said, "Did you hear me, Joaquin?"

"Yes," I said. "We'll be right down."

I got out of bed still wearing the Odd Fellow curtain over a T-shirt. D-Dog wasn't budging from the bed, though.

"Hey," I said to Mr. D.

He was lying on his side. He opened his eyes and looked at me but didn't move.

"If you're going to be up all night, you're going to be tired in the morning."

He stared at me from the bed.

"Mark wants us downstairs, so we have to go."

Mr. D. yawned.

As I put on some pants I said, "I'll get your cape."

D-Dog sleepily got up and walked to the edge of the bed.

"Wait. Wait," I said.

He looked at me lazily, with eyes half-closed, as I went and got his white cape from the dresser and Velcroed it to his collar.

"Okay, now you're ready for the day."

He jumped off the bed, and after I put on some tennis shoes and made a quick stop in the bathroom, we went downstairs. As we descended that huge staircase into the foyer, I didn't see Mark or Felix anywhere, so I went out onto the porch with Mr. D.

He was done rather quickly, not being fastidious about that sort of thing. He ran up the steps and we walked into the house together. Mark and Felix were waiting for us.

Mark said, "Do you have your gun?"

I motioned with my head as I said, "It's upstairs. In my room."

"Go get it." Mark continued, "Get your carpetbag, too."

He was referring to the carpetbag I had made out of a damaged second curtain that was thrown in (it had ripped in half) with the slightly moth-eaten one.

I started to ask why, but Mark was very firm as he cut me off and pointed. "Just go." He looked down at Mr. D. affectionately. "We'll watch D-Dog."

As I began my ascent up the stairs, he said, "Be careful."

How strange of him to say that. Mark has never been an alarmist. A libertine, yes, for he claims to follow his own path and for the most part he does, and he does have his own opinions concerning right and wrong. How many times have I've seen him bolt up after consuming too much alcohol and declare *I am a man about town!* to no one in particular; but an alarmist? No. Even after September 11, he was no alarmist.

The staircase was not built with the elderly or the infirm in mind. There must have been over a hundred steps just to the second floor, for the staircase was a technical marvel as it wound gradually and at a loping pace. As I proceeded down the hallway I noticed something I hadn't seen before—the faint traces of footprints. Animal footprints. They were much too large to be Mr. D.'s, and I suddenly understood why Mark seemed concerned.

I crept into my bedroom on the tips of my rubber-toed shoes. I located my gun where I had left it under my pillow and grabbed my holster from the bedpost. My carpetbag was in the wardrobe, so I moved silently to it and took it out. I only had to get out of the room and down the stairs to reach safety. At the doorway, I looked both ways and listened. I could hear the far-off murmuring of Felix and Mark and the clicking of D-Dog's toenails on the hardwood floors below. That was reassuring. Then I heard something else, an unusual movement that wasn't familiar, and some type of breathing. I ever so cautiously put on my holster, wrapping it around my waist slowly but with precision, not once looking down, and securing it under my Odd Fellows wool. I put the strap of my carpetbag over my head and the bag across my back so the bag lay upon the rear of my waist. I touched it to make sure it was closed and checked my gun to verify there were bullets in the chambers. There were; six chambers, six bullets.

I was set. It was time to flee, but I didn't want to leave the sanctuary of the present for the evil of the future. I wasn't going to move at all until I heard footsteps that didn't appear to be human. They came from one of the bedrooms down the hall. They had a muffled quality about them; a soft, smooth, unassuming quality. My plan was to run as fast—and as quietly—as I could, and if I was pursued I would grab on to the railing, pull myself over, and jump down to the foyer below. If I kept my gun in my hand I should be able to get off at least one shot before I was attacked.

Okay, I told myself, I would count down from ten, under my breath, and then run. I began: ten, nine, eight, seven, six, five, four, three, two...*one*. I didn't hesitate. I *ran*. I ran as fast as I've ever run. I sped down the hallway with my arms bent at the elbows, moving up and down quickly. I heard movement behind me and there was no turning back. I reached the staircase landing and jumped, left foot first, onto the first step, banging into the banister with my left hip before regaining my balance and then rapidly jumping down two steps. I took the staircase two steps at a time, jumping like a gazelle and moving faster than I've ever moved. Then the gunfire started.

Bullets ricocheted off the wall above me and behind me. The sound echoed off the walls in that huge open space. I could see Mark and Felix shooting at whatever was behind me, and all the while Mr. D. jumped up and down barking wildly. I aborted my plan to jump over the railing because there were too many bullets flying for me to jump anywhere safely. Out of the corner of my eye I could see up and above as bullets struck the wall, raining both plaster bits and dust in my direction. One of the beasts, climbing across the wall beside me, was hit by an array of bullets and fell onto the steps in front of me. He banged with a thud but the bullets continued to be fired, which meant one thing—there was more than one of them behind me. The wounded beast on the steps started to get up, so I shot my pistol. My arm jerked up from the force of the blast. I aimed as he looked directly at me with animal hostility and shot again. It hit him. I shot and hit him again; three bullets left and roughly thirty steps to go. From behind me a beast leaped past me, vaulted over the railing as I had planned to do, and landed on the floor of the foyer as I continued to race down the steps. It threw its head back and screeched before it headed toward Mark and Felix. D-Dog took off running toward the kitchen. Mark and Felix fired a thunderstorm of bullets into it. It screamed as it stumbled backward and fell to the ground in a wild and crazy display of inhuman emotion and action.

As I moved quickly to the final steps, Mark yelled, "To the kitchen! Go to the kitchen!"

I made it to the final step and my gauntlet seemed to be almost at an end when I was blindsided by one of the beasts. He plowed right into me from behind. I stumbled forward and fell to the ground on my back and slid upon the waxed floor only to stop in one big sprawl of symbols and limbs. The animal advanced toward me. I hid my head with the arm and hand that held the gun, but within a second of closing my eyes my right eye burst open and I looked up. It was standing over me, and it was obvious this was no time for timidity. I raised my gun and squeezed the trigger. I know I hit him, but my bullet was lost in the volley of bullets fired by Mark and Felix. As it stood above me I expected him to screech like the others but he did none of that; he appeared to be unsteady on his feet, and after teetering for the longest moment he fell over across my calves and feet. I lay beneath him for a flash of a second before jumping up and tearing off to the kitchen.

D-Dog was waiting for me. He barked when he saw me and his tiny tail wagged with relief as he danced about the floor. I bent down and picked him up.

The kitchen table was covered with layers of weapons: rifles upon rifles, handguns in piles, boxes of ammo stacked up in a haphazard way. Mark and Felix raced into the kitchen. Mr. D. didn't seem to mind. His body and tail perked up again and he began to wiggle anew. I could barely hold on to him, he was so excited.

I looked at him and said, "Am I going to have to medicate you?"

He stopped wiggling and looked at me with pursed lips. In an effort to placate me and to stop me from scolding him again he licked me slowly on the cheek, but strangely while he did this, he watched Mark and Felix out of the corners of his eyes.

Mark was all strategy from that moment on.

"Joaquin, put some of those guns in your carpetbag along with a flashlight. Load up on bullets, too. The .45s take the clips in the black box. Your gun takes the bullets in the yellow box."

He seemed impatient as I looked at the boxes. He stormed over to the table and put the right handguns with the right bullets and clips.

"Load up," he said. "Take as many as your bag can carry."

I did what he said because when Mark gets in *that* mood, you just do what he says. Mark loaded up his own backpack with bullets and handguns. I sat Mr. D. down on the table. He sniffed the boxes and the guns. Felix loaded up using Theodora's backpack.

There was a large window above the sink designed to let in light; that's where they burst in next. We saw it coming. One minute we were all around the table loading up with guns and ammo, and in the next instant glass from the window was headed toward us. It happened in slow motion, as we heard the sound and turned in unison to see glass flying about the room like little daggers, quickly followed by the appearance of a six-foot, hairy, snarling beast.

I grabbed D-Dog and the bag from the table and ran from the room. The kitchen erupted into gunfire. Mark and Felix were still shooting as they backed out hurriedly from the room and into me. I couldn't speak. My mouth was open and Mr. D. buried his face in my neck. Mark and Felix looked back and saw what I saw: more of them were coming toward us from down the hallway. We raced back to the kitchen but they were coming in through the window.

Felix's head whipped around and said, *"Aquí!"*

He pulled open a door that led downstairs to the basement. I didn't want to go.

Mark yelled, "Go!"

I didn't move.

He yelled at me, *"Get going, you little twit!"*

Scared, I took off down the pitch-black steps, but stopped halfway down and watched as Felix and Mark continued their shooting rampage. The animals screeched as they were hit, but I couldn't see any of it. Felix sprayed bullets toward the kitchen and Mark shot down the hallway. After two or three minutes there was quiet. Judging from the way their bodies relaxed I figured it was over. They both backed into the narrow staircase, Mark first and then Felix, who yanked the door closed. We were in total darkness.

"Where's the light switch?" I asked.

I heard a click and could see Felix standing on the top step holding a piece of cord attached to a bare lightbulb socket. He bolted the door shut.

"Why would there be a bolt on the inside of the door?" I asked.

Felix shrugged.

Mark looked at me with a scrunched-up nose, nodded, and said, "Good question, Joaquin.

"So what's down here?" he asked as he walked down the steps past me. He got to the bottom step, looked around, turned back to the three of us, and said, "Darkness. Darkness is down here."

"Tenemos luz. Let me show you."

Felix passed me on the steps and disappeared into the darkness. He started reaching into the air for pull strings. After he pulled the first one, it was easy to see the others. I worked up the courage and moved down to the bottom step. Mark had his back to me as he moved off to explore the basement.

I said, "You know…" but stopped.

Felix turned to look at me but Mark didn't.

I continued, "You know, Mark…"

He didn't turn around, so I tried again. "You know, I realize this is not the best time to bring this up, but I don't like being screamed at."

He stopped and without looking at me said, "I don't want to talk about it."

"I'm sure you don't," I said, "but I just want to make clear that I don't like being yelled at or being called names said in anger."

Mark did not respond.

"If I had parents I'm sure they wouldn't yell at me."

Mark turned around quickly. "I'm not your mother and I'm not your father." He walked up to me and poked me in the chest with one of his big, white fingers. "From now on, when I tell you to do something, *do it. Do you understand me?*"

I looked at him without responding.

"Do you want them to get Mr. D.?" Mark's eyes widened. "Do you?"

He looked at Mr. D. and then back at me.

"No," I said quietly as I averted my eyes from his.

Mark stood looking at me. I know he was. I could feel it.

"Okay, we're scaring Mr. D., so we have to stop," Mark said.

Mark made a goofy face, the one where he turns his head to the side, sticks out his tongue like Mr. D., and blinks his eyes. He made the face for me and Mr. D. Mark took him from me and cradled him like a baby in his arms and kissed him on the stomach. D-Dog always likes that. Mark carried him around the basement, rocking him. I moved closer to them to keep an eye on D-Dog.

With his back to me, Mark said, "You're very brave, Joaquin. You went first into all those spiders and snakes."

"Well," I said, "if I hadn't gone I think Felix would've pushed me, so…"

Mark made a growling noise that sounded like a cross between a pirate and a bear, which signaled to me that he had left our tiff behind and moved on.

"So, what's our plan?" I asked.

Mark growled again, this time with his mouth wide open and his tongue sticking out. I know Mark. He was trying to sound like a zombie, but he almost sounded like he was gargling.

In a slow "zombie-monster" voice that emphasized each word he said, "Try…not…to…get…killed."

Felix said, "I'm down with that, Señor Mark."

Mark continued speaking like a zombie. "Felix…down… with…da…plan…to…stay…alive."

"So, are we going back upstairs or are we staying down here?" I asked.

Mark reverted back to his oddball self and said chirpily, "I say we stay here for a while." He rocked his head from side to side in an exaggerated way before he said, "Let's see what's down here. Maybe there's a treasure in one of those boxes." He pointed to some of the cardboard and wooden boxes stacked about the basement.

"I don't know if we should go through that stuff," I said. "It doesn't belong to us."

Mark looked at me slightly annoyed. "Precious, we just shot up the foyer and kitchen. There are dead animals and blood all over the place. It doesn't matter what we do now. We're not getting *el deposito* back."

I thought about what he said. "Well, when you put it that way…"

We walked over to a wall of boxes and only had to open

one to realize it was a mistake. The first box Mark opened was cardboard. It was tied with rope and almost impossible to open. Thankfully, Felix had a switchblade on him.

When he undid the flaps and we could see inside the first thing I said was, "Why would someone put sugar in a box?"

Felix set me straight. "Drugs."

"I think we got some drugs here, my friends," said Mark.

I immediately said, "Close it up. We don't want to get in any trouble."

Mark looked at me and said, "Joaquin, have you been paying attention? Do you have your mind on straight? We're already in trouble. All we got is trouble. Trouble. Trouble. Trouble."

I stared at Mark and said, "This is no time to be singing show tunes."

"But it's about *Iowa*, Joaquin! Isn't that the place of your birth?"

When he said *Iowa* he moved his head up in a wavy, upside-down U motion as if his head and shoulders had just gone over a speed bump.

"No," I said. "I was born in Oklahoma."

He stood up and with a grand, sweeping man-about-town gesture flung his arms away from his body and burst out with one melodic word: *"Oklahoma!"*

Felix, having no knowledge of the American theater, looked completely confused. His response to Mark's outburst was totally understandable as he looked at me and asked, "Why would Señor Mark sing about this Oklahoma state?"

"Because he's a big, effete goofball."

"Oh," said Felix, but I could tell from his face that he was still confused and didn't understand.

With his arms still up in the air, Mark looked down at me

and said, "I deny being effete." He batted his eyelashes as he spoke, which kind of invalidated his denial.

"What do they grow in Iowa?" asked Mark. "Isn't it wheat?"

"No," I said, "that's Kansas."

"What do they grow in Iowa, then?"

"Corn."

"Oh, corn. I like corn," said Mark. "I always look exceptionally manly while I'm eating corn." He began to bite the air with his teeth as if he was eating corn. He didn't look manly. Rather, he looked like a plus-size beaver.

"And hogs," I said.

"Hogs?"

Mark's corn and hog thoughts were interrupted when Felix said, *"Qué es eso?"*

He pointed to the door. There was a small crack under the stairway door that allowed a glimmer of light to drift onto the top steps. That crack of light was being broken by shadows and movement. Mark turned to me. He pointed across the room to a door.

"What's that door?"

I shook my head.

"Find out," he said.

I looked at Mr. D. and said, "Come on."

Mark and Felix moved some of the boxes away from the wall and pushed them out toward the center of the room. I got up to the door and pulled on it. It didn't open. I yanked at the handle; nothing. The handle turned but the door wouldn't open. I examined the door more closely and realized that it was painted shut. I tried to wiggle it open but it wouldn't give. I turned to Felix.

"Felix, can I use your switchblade?"

Felix stood up from moving a box and looked at me. I pointed to the door.

"It's painted shut," I said.

Felix walked over and handed his switchblade to me. I had it in my hand and was trying to figure out how to open it when Felix said, *"Parado."*

He put his right hand beside my right hand and placed the switchblade in his own palm the "right" way. Then he depressed the tiny button that released the blade. He looked at me without saying anything and put the switchblade in my hand. I depressed the tiny button and it worked perfectly. I opened and closed it a couple of times to make sure I had it down. I did.

Felix looked at me with a faint smile on his face and said, *"Tenga cuidado."*

I used the switchblade to begin working on the painted door. I stood very close to it, intensely concentrating on my duty.

I started on the side closest to the handle. I inserted the blade and moved it with an up-and-down motion along the painted crack. The paint was old and chipped away rather easily. In no time at all I had done one complete side. I began working on the other side. There were layers and layers of paint. The topmost coat was a yellowish, dirty white, but almost all the other coats underneath were shades of red. I never realized there were so many different shades of red. The more I worked, the more it appeared as if the door was on fire. D-Dog sniffed the paint scrapings on the floor. He didn't like how they smelled, but he kept sniffing. I found the smell rather acidic and tried to hold my breath. I finished with the other side and looked for something to stand on so I could work on the top of the door. I pushed one of the boxes over to the door and just as I got it into place, just as I lifted up my right foot to step onto it, there was a huge *bang* at the top of the stairs. We all raced to the bottom step to look. Within seconds there was another enormous *bang* against the door. It was as if a huge log was being rammed into the door. The door shuddered. The hinges wavered. The lock rattled. We waited.

My eyes focused on the top hinge. Again, a huge force hit the door. I could see the hinge loosen and pop a little. We must have all seen it. In unison we all turned and scrambled back to our positions. I ran back to the other door, jumped up on the box, and started working on the top of the door. D-Dog moved lethargically toward me.

"What's wrong?" I asked.

He almost looked drunk. I frantically worked on the top of the door.

I looked back at him and again asked, "What's wrong?"

With an explosive blast, the stair door burst from its hinges. I turned my head to look and saw the door sail down the steps and bang against the opposite wall before clattering to the floor. It was followed by complete silence. The only thing moving was the dust in the air. I looked at Mark and Felix. They were crouched down behind the boxes in the center of the room with their automatic weapons aimed where the staircase door used to be. Mark looked at me and must have seen my fear. He smiled and winked at me. He pointed at Mr. D., who appeared to be asleep on the floor. *What's wrong with him?*

Mark pantomimed putting the blade in the crack and moving it back and forth. I didn't want to continue, I wanted to watch what was happening behind me, but Mark got a stern look upon his face and nodded forcibly. I went back to it. I had only just begun when I heard a screech from the top of the stairs. The sound scared me, and I turned my head back to look. All I could see was the hooved feet and the hairy legs of some creature on the second step from the top. I immediately jumped down from the box and scooped up Mr. D. He was totally asleep. I tried to wake him but he did not respond. I took the potion attached to his collar and held it up to him. His little black nose moved back and forth and he opened his eyes. I kissed him and he seemed to come out of his slumber. I held him close to my chest, in the crook of my arm, and petted his head as we watched and waited. We must have made quite a pair, me in my woolen drapery covered in symbols and Mr. D. in his cape. With my right hand I slowly took out my pistol and cocked it.

Mark and Felix started shooting as soon as the beast lifted one of its hooves, but it was fruitless. Within seconds, this beast, like none of the others, was upon them in one lunging, jumping movement. It landed on them and covered their bodies. I assumed the worst. They had to be dead. I ran with Mr. D. to a dark corner of the basement and shook my head. I stood with my back against the wall, trying to think of a way to save them. Mr. D. shook in my arms. I had no choice. I forced myself to run back. Felix and Mark fired an endless stream of bullets from beneath the animal.

The sound of their guns and their screams gave me hope.

I could not see either one of them and could not abdicate my responsibility no matter how frightened I was. I repeated the three links: *friendship, love, and truth; friendship, love, and truth; friendship, love, and truth.* God compelled me. I hastily put D-Dog on the ground and raced to the others.

Through clenched teeth I began, "Our father who art in heaven, hallowed be they name."

The beast lifted its head up. Blood gushed from its mouth. Its eyes were wide and filled with hostility.

"Thy kingdom come."

It threw its head back and screeched. Saliva dripped from its teeth.

"Thy will be done."

I did not hesitate. I held my arm out straight, but it still shook as I aimed at its face.

"On earth as it is in heaven. Give us this day our daily bread."

I shot twice and hit it once in the eye and once in the forehead. Its head jerked back as it was struck.

"And forgive us our trespasses as we forgive those who trespass against us."

Despite everything I had done to kill it, it still lunged at me.

"And lead us not into temptation."

I stumbled backward and fell onto the ground but lifted myself up onto my elbows. The beast lay before me motionless.

"But deliver us from evil."

There was complete silence.

"Amen."

I breathed heavily as I propped myself up. I could feel my heart beat. My crisscross of symbols heaved up and down upon my chest. D-Dog hesitantly walked over to me while keeping his eyes completely on the beast. He hid behind me and peered over my shoulder at its carcass.

There was the longest silence and then Mark, covered in blood, sat up and said, "Good shooting, Joaquin!"

Felix sat up and spat blood out of his mouth before he said, "*Muy bueno*. I thought we were, how do you say, goners?"

"Get up!" I said. "I don't know if it's dead yet."

Mark extricated himself from under its haunches with a disgusted look upon his face.

"Ewwww," he said as he stood up. He was covered in blood. He reached down and extended his hand to help up Felix. Mark used his palms to brush off his shirt but it didn't do any good. The blood remained.

He looked at me and Felix before he said, completely deadpan, "I'm covered in funky Chupacabras schmutz. Markie is not happy."

Felix wiped his face off with the backs of his hands. "No, Señor Mark, that was not the Chupacabras. None of them were the Chupacabras."

Mark looked at Felix, confused. It was then that Felix made a statement I found rather odd.

"They are soldiers in the Chupacabras's army."

"What?" Mark asked.

"We have not met the Chupacabras yet."

"Why do you say that?" Mark asked confused.

Felix glanced at the blood on his hands before looking up and saying, "I have seen the Chupacabras. When I was *un niño* El Chupacabras killed a man who worked for our family. I saw it. When we finally meet the Chupacabras, you will know. There will be no mistake."

Mark raised the index finger on his right hand and was already shaking it as if he was going to demand "a point of order," but was interrupted by a huge screech on the stairs.

Mark looked to the stairs and back at me. As he and Felix raced to retrieve their weapons he yelled, "Get that door open!"

I jumped upon my box and started working on the seal of paint at the top of the door. I worked in a hurried, frantic way, cutting away the paint and making the door redder. As it fell to the floor I rebuked D-Dog and told him not smell the paint chips. He looked at me rather puzzled but heeded my warning and was content to watch me and stay as close to my feet as he could by jumping upon the box.

They started to descend the stairs like an army in lockstep. I could see the lower extremities of the first two, then four, and then six. I knew we were in trouble. I frantically finished working on the top of the door. The entire door's casement looked like it was on fire. I jumped down off the box and yanked at the door handle. Nothing, nothing at all. I yanked again. I turned the handle to the left and then to the right. Mark and Felix backed toward me and Mr. D.

Mark said in a calm and steady voice, "How's that coming along, Joaquin?"

The beasts advanced on us. I turned the handle in a scramble, back and forth, back and forth.

I pleaded, "Please, God. Please, God."

There was a *click*. I caught my breath out of sheer relief and opened the door a crack to peer to the other side. Mr. D. scratched at the bottom of the door, trying to open it himself. I could see only steps and darkness.

"I don't know what's down there. There are wooden steps. It's dark. It's an enclosed staircase." My voice had a panicked tone to it.

"We're going," said Mark. "First you and D-Dog, then Felix, then me. Get down there, Joaquin. Get your flashlight out."

I reached around and fumbled in my bag for my flashlight. The beasts started emitting a hissing sound.

"Okay, I'm going. Come on, D-Dog."

He didn't need any prompting. He was already in front of me.

I aimed my flashlight down into the darkness but could see nothing but Mr. D.'s eyes looking back at me. I twisted back and shone the light on my side of the door.

"There's a lock. Like the other one," I said.

That was the last thing I said before the shooting started. All I could hear was gunfire and screeching.

At one point I heard Mark yell, "Over there!"

His voice startled me and my body jerked and involuntarily shivered. I scurried farther down the stairs. Mr. D. moved down the stairs, too.

I looked at him and said, "Stay here."

He had reached the floor next to the bottom step and moved around the way he does when he wants to take off running.

I said, "No. Stay here."

I heard loud thuds that appeared to be large animals hitting the concrete floor. It caused the staircase to shake. The repeated shooting from two guns eventually filtered down to the last bullets being fired from a single gun, and then there was silence. I heard no movement. I heard no voices. I heard no screeching. After about thirty seconds there was some muffled sound near the door, which was slightly ajar. Felix entered the stairwell backward with his gun still ready to shoot. As he moved toward me, I moved farther down the staircase.

My flashlight's stream of light went from the door's lock down to Mr. D., to make sure he hadn't taken off.

I heard Mark say, "Where's the frickin' light?"

I turned back to the doorway. The light's beam followed my arm's movement. I shone it across Mark's belly and pointed the light directly at the lock so Mark could secure it. He did, and the lock made a clunky *click* that sounded like hard steel banging together.

Mark looked at me and said, "Joaquin, can you point that flashlight down the stairs?"

I did as I was told. Mr. D. looked at us from the bottom step.

Mark waved and said, "Hey, D-Dog."

Mr. D. wagged his tail.

"Flash it toward the sides. I want to see what's over there."

I moved the flashlight's beam from side to side.

"Hmmm," said Mark.

I looked up at Mark and asked, "What?"

"Well, when you said there were stairs and darkness I just imagined different stairs and a different type of darkness."

"What does that mean?" I asked.

"Well, I didn't expect it to be so…dark."

I said, "Maybe if you guys pulled out your flashlights and turned them on, it wouldn't be so dark."

Mark squinted when he looked at me. I didn't know if it was because he couldn't see me or if it was because the light was in his eyes but eventually he said, "You're messing with me, aren't you, flashlight boy?"

"I'm simply making a suggestion," I said.

I could hear Mark mumbling under his breath. "Making a suggestion, huh? I'll give you a suggestion and it'll involve a fraternity paddle and you saying *ouch*. Now, where's my flashlight?"

He searched around in his backpack. Felix did the same. When everyone had their flashlights out and illuminated, the beams bouncing off the walls and low ceiling created a strange searchlight effect. The staircase ceiling was so low it was claustrophobic. As we made our descent Mark took the lead position, I was in the middle, and Felix took up the rear. Of course, D-Dog raced back up the steps to greet us as we walked toward him. It wasn't a long staircase. Not more than thirty steps. When Mark arrived at the bottom step he stopped. He extended his right arm to prevent us from moving forward. His flashlight's beam went first to the right and then to the left. I could hear water running off in the distance and there was an empty, hollow echo sound.

Some walls appeared to be made of concrete, and other walls were simply tunneled out of the indigenous stone. Mark extended both arms and motioned us to come forward. I went to Mark's right and Felix went to his left. Mark shone his flashlight down the tunnel again, first to the right and then the left.

"What do you think?" he asked.

I said, "Drug runners. Drug runners constructed this."

Mark looked at me and said, "You don't think it was constructed by coyotes for the trafficking of human cargo?"

"It could be used for that, too," I said. "It just depends on where the tunnel goes."

Felix chuckled. He played with his gun as he spoke. He had his index finger pointed straight out and twirled his gun on it like a gunfighter. I looked at him and thought, *Who is this? The Cisco Kid?*

"Mis amigos," he said, "this must lead to one place and only one place. It is our pathway there."

Being best friends and practically always in sync, Mark and I came to the same conclusion at the same time. Mark slapped his forehead in an overly animated way, moving his head back and forth as if he were a cartoon character who had just been hit in the head with an anvil.

With an open mouth and without moving his lips he looked at Felix and asked, "Which way?"

I could see on Felix's face that he was calculating where we were in relation to the first floor of Cascada.

"It has to be to the left," he said.

Mark had an unsure look on his face. He spoke normally when he said, "Let's go to the left," but didn't sound confident.

Mark and Felix stepped down from the bottom step onto the ground. There was a covering of fine dirt over what appeared to be standard-size clay bricks.

I said, "Wait."

They turned and looked at me. I hesitated before I spoke. I didn't really want to say it, but I felt compelled to be the voice of reason.

"Theodora can't be alive."

I'm sure I sounded like a coward to both of them. Mark got a soft look upon his face. He smiled and looked down at the ground and back up at me.

"You're right, Joaquin. She's probably dead. She was probably dead within an hour of being taken from us, but we have to check, don't we? We have to see for ourselves, right? Life is about friendship, love, and truth. I heard you say that yourself less than fifteen minutes ago. Could you live with yourself knowing that we didn't even try? Could you live with yourself not knowing whether or not she was alive or dead? The decision to go or not go is a fait accompli, my good friend. We must go."

I couldn't argue with that. "I just don't want anything to happen to the rest of us," I said.

"We'll be fine." Mark smiled. "We're three tough guys

and one tough dog." Mark looked down at Mr. D. "Right, D-Dog?"

D-Dog made a nasal sound and then sat down on his rear, licked between his toes, and chewed on one of his toenails.

Mark pointed at D-Dog. "See, D-Dog isn't scared. He's giving himself one of those dog pedicures right in the middle of all of this."

Mark tilted his head to the left to urge me on. "Come on, man. Let's go find Theodora."

I stood motionless. I certainly didn't want to go. I lifted my right foot off the step. It felt like it weighed a thousand pounds. I set it down on the ground. I lifted my left foot, and it only felt like five hundred pounds.

I looked down at Mr. D. and said, "Let's go, D-Dog."

Mr. D. stood up and the four of us walked down the pitch-black tunnel together—our flashlights beacons, searching out the unknown.

❖

Felix said, "*Uno o dos* kilometers at most."

I nodded at his estimation but felt this was a mistake. I once read a recommendation that people trust their instincts; that their instincts wouldn't lead them astray and would warn them when danger was around the next corner or knocking at the door. My instincts told me this was a colossal misstep and we should turn back. I held my tongue, though. I didn't want Mark to think less of me. I wanted to be the man he saw me as, even if it bore little resemblance to the scared little *hombre* I knew I was.

After about ten minutes, we arrived at a spot that appeared

to be not as well constructed as the rest of the tunnel. This section was held up by large, wooden beams along the walls and across the ceiling. It reminded me of an abandoned mine.

The floor was uneven. Clay bricks in a symmetrical pattern gave way to dirt. The dirt was loose and three or four inches deep, so it was like walking in black snow. There were large holes throughout it and I wondered if Don Humberto had a mole problem. The walls, supported by beams, were perfect for cobwebs, which became our nuisance. They were not constructed by the large, bird-eating spiders of the day before, but they were still spiders, and their constant scurrying at our approach or from the light of our flashlights or when we broke through one of their webs had me constantly brushing off my shoulders.

I probably looked like I had an obsessive-compulsive disorder. Mark and Felix didn't seem to have any issue with the cobwebs or the spiders. Mr. D. occasionally walked into a web and tried to dislodge it from his fur by rolling around in the dirt, at which point we would stop and wait for him. As we moved through this bit of the tunnel, the ceiling got lower and the path became narrower. We progressed at a slower pace as the tunnel turned less accessible, and it was in this area that we found the first body. Mr. D. noticed it before the rest of us. I knew something was amiss when he stopped and began to growl. I directed my flashlight to where he looked. It was one of those beasts. It had been dead so long and was subsequently so rigid that it appeared petrified. It was an emaciated body covered in coarse fur.

Felix kicked it lightly in the head to see if he would get any response. It didn't move.

"Muy muerto," said Felix.

D-Dog walked up to it growling, was obviously wary

of it, but had to sniff it all the same. Mark made a growling noise as Mr. D. sniffed, which made him jump back, look at Mark, and bark twice. I didn't need any dog translator to know what Mr. D. was saying. He raced over to Mark, grabbed the bottom of a pant leg with his teeth, and pulled back and forth, shaking his head from side to side as he growled. Mark bent down and picked him up. He kissed him about the head, but Mr. D. was in no mood to be kissed. He *allowed* himself to be kissed but turned his head away from Mark and snubbed him. Mark would not give up. That was not in Mark's nature. He continued to kiss D-Dog and then he cradled him in his arms and kissed him on the belly. D-Dog squirmed, of course, and that did it. He and Mark were once again best friends as D-Dog scrambled up to lick Mark about the face.

As we moved forward, there were more bodies of dead beasts and something that wasn't a welcome sight to see— human remains. Two men. One was sprawled on the floor where he'd fallen, a bullet hole through his back. Hardened blood, dried years ago, surrounded the wound.

The other one was sitting with his back against the wall. Felix shone his flashlight's beam on him. He was wearing what appeared to be a military uniform. His skin was tight and dry with a gray pallor, and he had no eyes left in his sockets. A gun lay on the ground beside him, and he held in his hand a slightly crumpled piece of parchment paper. Mark bent down and pulled it from his rigid fingers. He stood up, turned the piece of paper over, straightened it out a bit, read it, and smiled uncomfortably. He handed it to me and said, "Read it for Felix."

I took the paper from him, set my flashlight upon it, and read the scrawled words in a loud, clear voice: "Welcome. The entrance you are seeking is straight ahead."

I handed the paper to Felix and asked, "Do you think it was intended for us or just for anybody?"

Mark moved his head back, smirked, and said, "Does it matter?"

"Well, if we're heading into an ambush I would like to have a plan ready."

Mark walked up to me and poked me in the chest. "Shoot 'em and kill 'em. That's our plan. Then shoot 'em and kill 'em again to make sure they're dead." He turned away from me and looked off into the distance. The beam of his flashlight scanned the darkness.

"It can't be much farther," he said. He turned back to us. "Come on. Let's go. I'm antsy."

No one moved.

Mark looked down at Mr. D. "Come on, buddy." He slapped his thighs lightly with the palms of his hands.

Mr. D. walked up to Mark and the two of them started out. Felix glanced at me before he walked around the dead man, bent down and slipped the paper back between his dead fingers.

He stood up and said, *"Vámanos."*

I looked in Felix's eyes, which were barely visible in the darkness. I'll say this much for Felix—he isn't as hard as Mark.

"Estará bien," he said.

We walked maybe another kilometer. The more we walked, the narrower and more claustrophobic the tunnel became. Mark and Felix were crouching over when we finally reached the end, which thankfully opened up so the two of them could stand up straight again. The only way to continue was to climb through a small crawl space in the wall. It was approximately five feet off the ground and maybe three feet by three feet square. We peered through the opening and were able to see to the other side. We could only see some stairs. Though we couldn't see water, there was an unmistakable moving reflection.

Mark said, "I'll go first."

I pointed my flashlight from the crawl space to Mark and said, "Uh, Felix will fit through. I'll fit through and Mr. D. will fit through. Do you think…" I almost finished my sentence before Mark placed his flashlight under his chin and illuminated his face.

He appeared offended as he said, "What are you insinuating?" I began to explain but Mark cut me off again. "You're insinuating that I'm fat, aren't you?" Mark squinted at me. "You think my big body *and big man ass* won't fit through that tiny hole, don't you?'

I opened my mouth to speak but I didn't get a chance.

"Just because I'm husky and a grown-ass man doesn't mean I can't fit through that tiny space."

I held up my arm as if I was in grade school. "Can I speak?" I asked.

Mark looked at me and said, "No. Class is over and I have to grade papers. Guess who's getting a big, husky F?"

I worked up my courage to say, "Well, I'm going to speak anyway."

Mark folded his arms in front of his chest. His flippant mood had turned sour.

"What I was going to say was your backpack is so bulky it will most certainly catch on the top of the crawl space. You should take it off and push it in front of you."

Felix looked at Mark and his backpack. "*Sí*, he's right."

"Oh, and another thing. Since I can't swim and we don't know how deep the water is, I say Felix goes first, then D-dog, *you*, then me. If the water's deep I'm going to hold on to you as you swim. *You* can help *me* if we do it this way."

Mark stared at me with pursed lips.

"So make sure you wait for me after you jump in."

Mark scrunched up his nose and pursed his lips more.

"And finally, I will always be on your side, Mark, just as I always expect you to be on my side."

I paused so some of this could sink into that big 2X-sized brain of his.

Mark had a peculiar look on his face, the kind he gets when he's stumbled into a faux pas. It's a combination of embarrassment and petulance. Of course, he didn't say *forgive me* or *I'm sorry*. Those phrases aren't in Mark's vocabulary. Instead he simply said, "Well, fiddle-dee-dee," in an attempt to brush the whole matter aside with a smile and fake gaiety. I was in no mood to get into another tiff with the person who would soon be my life preserver, so I let the matter resolve itself by keeping my mouth shut.

Felix took off his backpack. He looked at both of us as he held it up. "This won't float. The guns are too heavy. Slip it over one arm before you jump."

Mark and I both nodded. Felix shoved his backpack into the hole. He had his flashlight in one hand and a pistol in the other. He set them down in the crawl space an arm's length away. He pulled himself up into the space. He had to balance himself, half in and half out. He pulled himself forward, collected both gun and flashlight, and pushed the backpack forward. He began to maneuver himself through the space.

"Be careful," I said. I clenched my fists and walked around in a circle impatiently.

Mark yelled into the crawl space, "Can you see anything?"

Felix's voice was muffled when he said, *"Nada."*

I put Mr. D. up into the crawl space so he could watch Felix and know what we were doing. The crawl space appeared to be under fifty feet long, so we waited anxiously for Felix to get to the other side. It took him no time at all—under five minutes.

In a difficult-to-decipher voice he yelled back, "It's thirty to thirty-five feet down to the water."

We peered into the crawl space at him. We could see him put his flashlight in his bag, but he kept his gun out. He slipped the backpack over one arm and then there was a pause.

"Is he going to go face first?" I asked.

Mark kept his eyes on Felix. "He doesn't have a choice."

For the longest second we didn't see any movement—then face first he crawled out of the space and was gone. We waited to hear the splash.

I counted out loud, "One, two, three, four, five, six..."

There was a loud splash. We could hear movement in the water.

In under a minute he yelled back, "Okay, go."

His voice sounded far away.

Mark repeated Felix's pre-crawl actions precisely. I don't think Mr. D. knew what he was supposed to do. He wanted to get out of the crawl space but Mark pushed him back and said, "You're going too, mister."

Mark hoisted all two hundred and twenty-five pounds of himself up and into the crawl space. He made a big *oomph* sound as he flattened out onto his belly. He slowly pulled himself forward, all the while pushing his backpack, shining his flashlight, and coaxing D-Dog to keep moving.

I watched him for a minute, turned back, and glanced into the dark tunnel. Looking back at me were a series of small beady eyes—in the bodies of small tiny animals. They were what I would have imagined the Chupacabras to look like from firsthand accounts, drawings, and photographs. There were a number of them, twenty or more. When I flashed my light at them they began to make a chattering noise.

Slowly, I took an automatic weapon out of my carpetbag. I looked into the crawl space. Mark was halfway through. I very cautiously lifted myself up and into the opening. Once in, I was small enough and short enough to work my way around in the space so I was still facing them. Mark, Felix, and D-Dog had gone face first through the crawl space. I was going feet first. I could hear Mark's grunts and D-Dog's pants as I moved backward toward them, all the time keeping my eyes, flashlight, and gun on those tiny little animals.

The lot of them approached the crawl space wall, hesitant at first, but they quickly became bold. Mark was still ahead of me with D-Dog when the first one jumped up into the crawl space. It hopped up with the dexterity of a fluffy squirrel and took tentative steps toward me. I continued to move backward, away from it. The first one acted like a domesticated pet, making cute soft noises, and almost appeared to smile in a harmless manner.

That is, until it heard me cock the trigger on my weapon, at which point it slowly turned its head directly toward me. Its eyes widened with intense animal fury and it let out a crazy, loud-pitched screech before it scurried like an oversized rat toward me. I had learned one important lesson in the last three days: don't hesitate. I started shooting.

I heard Mark say "What the..." in between shots, but I didn't look back at him.

I simply yelled, "Go! There are about twenty of them!"

Another one scrambled over the body of the first and came

at me; fifty pounds of sharp teeth and nasty, mange-covered rage. I shot again. He lunged at me as I continued to fire my gun. He didn't get very far before I hit him with bullets but he continued on even after he was hit. This one came perilously close as it fell in front of me with a dead-weight thud.

"Hurry, Mark," I yelled. There was a great deal of anxiety in my voice.

"I'm at the edge," he said, trying to comfort me.

"Get going!"

Another one scurried down the crawl space. On its way to me it stopped and sniffed the two already shot. Their dead state seemed, to use a phrase Mark has used in the past and which I would be reluctant to say out loud, to "piss him off."

"What's the holdup?" I yelled as I shot the animal between the eyes.

It fell backward with a squeal and a big thump.

"D-Dog doesn't want to go."

"Make him!"

I don't know what Mark did because I couldn't see, but within seconds Mark said, "We're out of here!"

I counted, "One, two, three, four..." and heard a *huge* splash of water.

"Come on, Joaquin," Mark yelled from below.

His voice sounded hollow.

My goal was to turn around in the crawl space in order to jump face first, but there wasn't time. Those little animals were on a mission to get me at any cost. They were all sharp teeth and anger propelling themselves over their dead brethren to *get me!*

My feet were out of the crawl space and dangling above what I assumed to be water. One of the crazed animals jumped at me, his face contorted and his mouth open, *shrieking*. I fired my gun as I pushed myself out and away from the crawl space. I must have been quite a sight, draped in all my symbols, as I fell backward through the air shooting at the tiny Chupacabras animals. The room I fell into was enormous—at least half the size of a football field—and the ceiling had to be a hundred feet high. Covering all the walls were ancient Aztec symbols. I kept shooting as I fell to the water. More and more of the animals jumped from the crawl space after me. I hit the water with a splash and could see the animals continue to jump from the tiny opening through the wavy water above me. Something grabbed me. I didn't know what it was at first and then recognized it as Mark's arm.

His watery, muffled voice said, "I've got you. I've got you."

He pulled me up from the water and I gasped for air. My chest heaved. I couldn't breathe. I coughed and spat out water. He pulled me along and all the while I heard gunshots from somewhere in the room as they echoed in that enormous, cavernous space. As Mark pulled me along I looked beside myself and saw Mr. D. dog-paddling, his cape spread out over the water's waves. He looked at me and barked.

❖

Felix was doing all the shooting. I was looking forward to getting out of the water. It was fast becoming a floating graveyard of dead *"pequeño"* beasts, and while the water wasn't too clear to begin with, now I really didn't want to be submerged in it any longer than necessary. We were quickly at the rocky shore. When I could stand in the water, I turned and watched as D-Dog climbed out and shook himself. Mark looked worn out from saving me.

As we emerged I put my hand on his shoulder and said, "Thank you."

He nodded in acknowledgment and said in a raspy voice, "Anytime." He took a long breath.

The crazed small animals had stopped jumping from the crawl space. The opening looked inordinately small from the other side of the vast room; it was strategically placed in the mural so they had appeared to be jumping out of the mouth of who I would later learn via Felix was Chalmecatecuchtlz, the Aztec god of the underworld and of sacrifice.

The steps that led out of the room were much larger than they appeared to be through the narrow slit of the crawl space. These concrete steps had all the dignity of American courthouse steps, but were much higher and wider. While we only walked down thirty steps from the basement of Cascada to the tunnel beneath, we'd obviously walked downhill through the tunnel. As the four of us stood before the massive and overwhelming steps I estimated there to be seventy or eighty, at least.

There was no place to go but up. The steps were too high for Mr. D. to climb. They were too high for me to climb, too. Since there was no handrail and I didn't have the balance or coordination to walk up the steps unaided, I had to think of an alternative. The steps were between twenty-four and thirty inches in height. I found it much easier to sit on the step and swing my legs up and around and place them on the step I was sitting on. I could then stand up, sit down on the next step and repeat the procedure all over again. This was much more involved than just walking up the stairs, but somebody had to carry Mr. D. Mark couldn't do it—he was too busy spending all his energy trying to keep up with Felix.

As I proceeded up the steps behind Mark and Felix, I looked around the room. It was peculiar. The basic separate parts reminded me of a high school gymnasium: the high ceiling, the pool area, the steps leading down to the water. The walls weren't concrete but either stone or rock sheered to an almost flat surface, but irregularities still existed. Excavating the space of dirt and rock must have been an enormous feat. The actual Aztecs couldn't have done it—it's too far north for them, and they would have been exterminated by the Spanish by the time this structure was built. It was constructed by someone who admired them. The light in the room entered via a series of large skylights in the center of the ceiling.

The murals on the walls were faded, the colors no longer vibrant due to their age and the constant harsh sunlight upon their surface. They weren't true depictions of Aztec symbols. They were an artist's interpretation of the symbols. They reminded me of the murals at the Detroit Institute of the Arts.

Including breaks, we took about twenty minutes to get to the top of the staircase, which terminated about fifteen feet beneath the ceiling.

It was here where the worst thing that could have happened occurred.

At the top of the stairs there was a colonnade. The columns were all perfectly white and all perfectly wrong. There *should* have been stone columns depicting Aztec gods.

Felix and Mark were standing on the edge of the landing when I got to the top with D-Dog. They were discussing the murals, Mark lamenting that he didn't have his camera. Exhausted, I sat D-Dog down on the top step and he scampered up to Mark. I walked over to join Felix and Mark as D-Dog walked along the colonnade. Out of the corner of my eye I saw movement. I turned to see more clearly, and as I turned Mark and Felix looked back, too. Their heads moved together—like brothers. Mr. D. stopped and stared at the three of us. His tiny tail wagged. His face lit up. His cape was nearly dry.

From behind a column a large animal arm reached out. It moved with precision straight toward D-Dog.

I immediately yelled, "Run, Mr. Dangerous, *run!*"

As I raced toward him, the hand swooped down and grabbed him by the scruff of his neck. I stopped. The hand raised him into the air. D-Dog began to whimper and squirm. His little legs moved as he tried to get away. He tried to bark but no sound came out. Felix and Mark raced up and flanked me with their guns cocked and ready to fire.

Felix said under his breath, "I'll shoot it in the arm."

He aimed, but there was nothing left to shoot.

The arm and D-Dog were gone.

X.
MARK CROWDEN'S BLOG: THE BRIDE

We ran to the columns—guns ready—but there was no sign of them. Little Joaquin was inconsolable. He raced back and forth to nowhere in particular. I know he was trying to hold it together because of Felix, but he finally just put his hands over his face and burst into tears. It was awkward for all of us. First Theodora, then Lord Leighton, and now D-Dog; these annoying Chupacabras suckers reminded me of a boil I once had in the crack of my ass. I couldn't get Joaquin to stop crying, and it was taking an awful long time for him to man up, so I had to play the only card I had left in the deck—the faith card. I gave him a big bear hug, lifting him up off the floor as I did. I sat him down on a step and put my arm around his shoulder and reminded him that he's always praying.

"I see you pray more than anyone else I've ever known."

Joaquin listened.

"I assume you pray because you believe in God and believe he will answer your prayers, right?"

Joaquin looked at me teary-eyed and nodded.

"If you believe in God you must have faith in him." I moved my head up and down slightly. "You have to have faith in God now, today, this minute."

Joaquin listened to me.

"This is when your faith must be the strongest. We don't know that D-Dog is dead, or Theodora, for that matter."

I hugged him tightly around the shoulder and brought him closer to me. "You have to believe that God will protect D-Dog and keep him safe. God will not forsake you, Joaquin, but you have to have faith."

I looked him in the eyes and asked, "Do you have faith? Do you believe God will protect D-Dog?"

Joaquin nodded and teared up again. I hugged him as tight as I could and helped him stand up.

"Okay, we have to go. Sitting here isn't going to bring anybody back."

He stood with his head bowed.

"Come on." I grabbed him by the wrist and pulled him along with me.

I looked at Felix and asked, "Which way?"

Without saying a word Felix led us down a path between the Doric columns farther and farther into the house. The columns served the function of walls to a maze. Like the path they enclosed, they wound and continued one way, then another. The actual path beneath our feet was constructed of rectangular red paving stones with a metallic sheen that reflected our bodies. It curved and dropped as it went along—curved again and again and then still again till we were underground once more. Every tenth pillar had a torch attached to it, and the glowing light threw our shadows in a multitude of directions as we ran. We turned a sharp corner and the columns were replaced by walls constructed of large bricks made of yellow sandstone. These walls continued on and on and on and on for a maddening eternity before they were replaced by clinker brick. We ran through all of it. I pulled Joaquin along when he didn't want to continue and raced to keep up with De La Santos. The clinker brick walls abruptly terminated at a dead end: a huge red door set into the mouth of a stone serpent. In the center was a painted image of a clenched fist holding a dagger. This was our entrance.

As we caught our breath I looked at Felix with his big guns and thought, *Felix De La Santos is one confident guy.* He walks around with his gun cocked, ready to shoot, and I have yet to see him afraid of anything.

He turned and looked at Joaquin and me. He gave us the up and down—the once-over, calculating our ability to assist him—before he tapped the barrel of his gun to his forehead.

He smiled at us as he asked, "*Hombres,* are you ready to kill El Chupacabras?"

He said it with a great deal of enjoyment in his voice. *He said it like the Chupacabras is something tasty to order at a Mexican restaurant.* I felt myself nodding, but I'm sure I didn't do it very persuasively.

I looked at Joaquin, who appeared withdrawn.

He was mumbling to himself as I said, "Get your gun out."

Joaquin did not respond, so I pulled his gun out of its holster and put it in his hand. I glanced at Felix and tried to look encouraging, but Joaquin and I at the serpent's door appeared to be pretty pathetic backup killers.

"Okay, we're ready," I said.

Felix smiled. He pointed at me and said, "I'm counting on you, Señor Mark."

He turned back to the door. His gun held straight out in front of him, he pushed the door open with the gun's barrel. The door creaked. Felix took a step forward and Joaquin and I followed. Before us was an enormous and amazing Aztec interior. It was bigger than the other space with the water and murals, and this space looked unreal, but not for any of the reasons one would expect. Being an architectural historian I knew this space had to be constructed between 1925 and 1940. It was Aztec art deco and it was spectacular.

As we stood in the doorway I whispered to Joaquin out of the corner of my mouth, "Keep an eye out for D-Dog."

The room appeared to be the approximate size of a small ocean liner in height, depth, and width. There was a large pyramid in the center of the room with steps on all four sides. Beside the main pyramid were two smaller pyramids that appeared to be lopped off near the top; they almost came to a point but didn't. Light emanated from the tops of these pyramids, but we would have to climb higher or climb the pyramids themselves to find out the light source.

Painted in muted dark colors, all four walls were covered in Aztec symbols, and they looked like they were painted by José Orozco. The room was enormously high and at various levels there were iron catwalks attached to the walls; each catwalk had its own entrance and exit. In a large niche above one of the catwalks was an old Hammond organ. It looked big enough for a movie theater and had a spotlight trained on it.

We walked farther into the site and discovered, off to the left, a large three-sided room, maybe fifty feet square, with a ceiling at least twelve feet high. Attached to the walls within this space were stainless steel counters, and there were numerous large stainless steel islands. Hanging above the counters and islands were charts, graphs, and diagrams, all related to animals: their evolution, their anatomy, and their reproductive systems. The counters were covered with computers, glass beakers, sinks, experiments in progress, hot plates, and all the other accoutrements associated with a scientist's laboratory. Don Humberto appeared to be following in the irregular footsteps of all the mad scientists who had preceded him.

I stood back and used my right index finger to move through some charts on one of the tables. I sniffed when I noticed something about dogs and genetic engineering, then quickly used my whole hand to fan the charts back to their original position before Joaquin noticed. He didn't need to see that. After a quick survey of the room I came to the conclusion that Don Humberto was interested in genetic engineering, animal experimentation, and per some explicit graphics hanging from the ceiling, human sacrifice. I realized Theodora was not destined to be the bride of the Chupacabras or Don Humberto, for that matter. A far more terrible fate had awaited her.

There was a humming coming from within the room. The sound came from tubular fluorescent lights attached to the iron catwalks. There was no other sound with the exception of the rustlings sounds we made. I could hear myself breathing.

I turned to Joaquin and asked, "Did you bring any water?"

He opened up his carpetbag and pulled out a bottle of water. Felix looked at me. I gave it to him first. He unscrewed it and took a drink and then I had some. I screwed the cap back on and returned it to Joaquin.

I said, *"Ahhhhh,"* big and loud.

Joaquin looked at me like I was an idiot or he was upset with me or he understood why I would always be a confirmed bachelor.

I pointed to one of the pyramids and asked him, "What do you think's up on those platforms?"

He shrugged. "I say we go and look."

Felix nodded, so we headed over to the base of the closest pyramid where Felix said, *"Permanezcan aquí."*

He used his index finger to point at the ground. It sounded like a good idea, so I nodded.

Joaquin began to climb the pyramid the normal way but found it too difficult, so he climbed it with his feet sideways instead. Joaquin, who is a tiny, jumping elf compared to me, was much better at this than I was. In no time at all he had put seventeen steps between us.

"Hey," I said, "not so fast."

I couldn't do it the way Joaquin was doing it. My feet were too wide. I was actually climbing up the pyramid the regular way. Facing the steps, I held on to the step at eye level while I raised my foot beneath me.

When Joaquin reached the summit I heard him gasp before he said, "Oh, my God, Mark. Come quick!"

"What is it?" I asked.

"I can't tell you. You have to come and look," he said.

With my big ass sticking out into the air *and no one around to admire it*, I continued up the pyramid, and when I could finally see the top of the platform, I realized why Joaquin was excited: Mr. D., of course, lay on the platform at the top of the pyramid. The platform was no bigger than six feet by six feet and constructed of thick glass that somehow seemed to float above a water source. The glass and water were illuminated by artificial lights. I watched as D-Dog appeared to be coming out of a Chupacabras-induced slumber via the Countess's *poción*. I don't know which of them looked happier: Joaquin or D-Dog.

As D-Dog continued to sniff his way back to the realm of the living, Joaquin asked, "So, what's on the other platform?"

I did a backward glance and could see Theodora, lying flat on her back like a princess. She floated silently above the water. Her hair was perfectly arranged and her arms were down at her sides. Her robe looked immaculately pressed and straight.

We began our descent.

"Look who we found," I said to Felix.

At which point Joaquin lifted D-Dog into view and Felix said, *"Su perro!"*

Joaquin beamed all the way down. I don't ever remember him being happier.

When we arrived back at the base, I said to Felix, "Theodora's up on the other pyramid."

He pointed to it and said, *"Aquí?"*

I nodded.

"Let's go get her," he said.

He forcefully led the way. There was a determined look on his face, and he was singularly focused on retrieving Theodora. We had the pyramid in our sights when a door on the opposite side of the room opened with a hollow clang. We all instinctively moved back against the wall and blended in. I couldn't see who walked through the door, but my eyes searched the sound area. I was able to pinpoint the guy with a guitar stumbling along the catwalk. He made a great deal of noise and looked rather sickly. He ventured down a flight of cast-iron stairs, which caused me to lose sight of him.

Felix whispered, "That's Enrique the guitar man."

A few seconds later the guitar man was followed by Loca Rosa, who wore a strange hoop-skirt contraption and a peculiar hat and carried a basket.

"Isn't she supposed to be dead?" I asked.

Felix nodded and gave me a confused look. Crazy Rosa threw flower petals about the base of the middle pyramid. She ascended the steps in an awkward, lethargic, and unenthusiastic manner as she tossed the petals about. I'm almost sure they weren't being scattered due to some involuntary twitch on her part, but another part of me thought she didn't even know what she was doing. She acted like a pot head who was pushed out a door and told to do "it" but didn't really understand what she was supposed to do.

Then it got weird.

One of the large, hairy beasts—the ones that tried to kill Joaquin on the staircase—appeared on the catwalk. It crawled up the stairs of the pyramid Theodora rested on. Felix aimed his gun and was ready to shoot, but I reached out, grabbed his gun, and pushed it toward the ceiling.

"Wait," I whispered. "They haven't killed her in two days. They're not going to kill her, suddenly, now—right?"

He squinted his eyes and looked at me before hesitantly lowering his gun. We watched the beast make its way up the pyramid gorilla-like, scoop up Theodora, and thrust her over its shoulder. It hurried down the pyramid and proceeded up the middle one.

As the beast walked up the steps, the top section of the pyramid—the part containing the eye on the back of an American dollar bill—mechanically rose up and tilted so the square base of the pointed section and the square top of the pyramid's platform intersected at a ninety-degree angle. The pointed part of the pyramid, obviously, wasn't stone because it then retracted into itself to create a walk-through opening, a doorway, that allowed entrance onto the platform. The beast pulled Theodora off its shoulder and held her in its outstretched arms. It stood before this newly created doorway and waited. The platform of the pyramid opened at the center and slid down into the sides like the tambour of a rolltop desk. Then a wood altar rose, bringing along with it a new floor to support the altar. When all the locking mechanisms stopped, the beast carried Theodora over the threshold of the doorway and set her down on the altar.

I didn't like where this was going.

Don Humberto appeared in one of the catwalk's doors. He was being pushed in a wheelchair by Enrique. The two of them slowly moved along the iron catwalk to the base of the pyramid Theodora slumbered upon.

Don Humberto's frailty was evident. He wore a mask over his face. It was a distorted version of Huitzilopochtli, a war god, according to Felix. His hands shook as if he had Parkinson's disease and his age was indeterminable.

Enrique knelt down in front of Don Humberto's wheelchair and said, "Magistral, I am your slave. We will take you to her."

He said it in a cloying and subservient manner that brought a nauseous, scrunched-up look to my face and made me think I might vomit.

A door on the catwalk opened with a loud echo and a bang. Two beasts walked out with metal rods in their hands. They marched to Don Humberto's wheelchair. Like clockwork they inserted the rods into Humberto's chair. One of the rods was screwed into the tires' hubs, the other to a soldered rod secured behind the leg rests. With a beast on each side of the wheelchair and nestled between the bars, they reached down.

With their left hands they grasped the back bar; with their right they grasped the front bar. They raised the chair and waited.

Enrique climbed up on the organ stool and after a dramatic flourish began to play: Carl Orff's "O Fortuna" from *Carmina Burana*.

The beasts began their ascent in lockstep—right foot first. I was amazed that they could walk with such rigid assuredness up the steps.

Our eyes were momentarily diverted to a door, which was flung open. It banged against the painted stone wall. Through this doorway Crazy Rosa, in 1970s platform shoes, reappeared and stepped out onto the catwalk in all her hoop-skirted glory.

She made hesitant steps and slowly lifted her arms, watching her open hands as they passed in front of her face. She looked at them as if she didn't know what they were, as if they were aliens attached to her body. She moved her arms about her head and proceeded down the catwalk. So consumed was she by her own movement that Crazy Rosa appeared unaware of the beasts moving up the stairs adjacent to her performance art.

Felix raised his gun as the beasts moved up the pyramid. I knew it was time, so I looked at Joaquin. He held D-Dog in his arms. I raised my gun, closed one eye, and aimed.

The unholy trinity reached the top of the platform and stopped. Don Humberto carefully stood up after exerting a great deal of effort.

Felix fired his pistol and as I saw him pull his trigger, I pulled mine.

Felix's target fell over onto its back and slid down the stairs dead. Mine was wounded and reached for its neck to stop the blood from gushing out. The wheelchair rolled down the steps backward and crashed against the wall at the bottom. As Felix and I took off running toward the pyramid, I caught a glimpse of Joaquin emptying the contents of his carpetbag. The bullets and guns made an enormous noise as they hit the floor. I didn't stop to ask why, and soon he was racing up the pyramid's steps, too. His carpetbag was not slung over his back as it normally was but instead was slung onto his chest, with Mr. D. inside. His head stuck out of the bag, and judging from the look on his face, he appeared to enjoy being there.

Having done it once, and with adrenaline racing through my body now, the pyramid steps weren't nearly as difficult. I also realized that these were much wider than the steps on the other two pyramids. The beast I'd shot in the neck stumbled down the steps and passed us on our way up. It almost seemed human as it looked at me in the eyes. I didn't shoot it again and put it out of its misery. Don Humberto raised his shaky hand high in the air. He held in his grasp an object that was shiny and sharp. It looked like he was going to bring down his arm and strike Theodora with it but he dropped whatever it was and it fell a few feet away.

Doors on the catwalk burst open and an army of beasts stormed toward us. Felix and I began shooting as Joaquin continued up the steps. Don Humberto held on to the wooden altar as he cautiously bent down to grab the shiny object. He wheezed as he bent down; he reached for the object, which was just out of his grasp. His fingers strained to grab it.

Joaquin made it to the altar and would later describe the object to Felix. Felix said it was an *obsidian*, an ancient Aztec tool used in human sacrifice. Joaquin tried to pull Don Humberto's hand off the altar, but Don Humberto would not let go. Joaquin aimed his gun at him but didn't shoot. Don Humberto, Joaquin would later claim, turned and looked at him. Through the mouth of the mask he could see a faint smile appear on his wrinkled lips. Joaquin said it seemed benign at first, but the longer he looked, the more evil the smile became. Joaquin pulled Felix's switchblade from his own back pocket, flicked it open, raised his arm—high into the air—and brought down the knife. It pierced Don Humberto's hand and stuck in the wooden altar. Don Humberto screamed in a frail, barely audible voice. He gasped for air.

Joaquin covered his nose with his hand. D-Dog buried his face in Joaquin's chest. The foul smell coming from Don Humberto's wound was horrific. Joaquin ran to the other side of the altar and bent over Theodora. He used the *poción* from the countess to revive her. Theodora opened her eyes. She seemed disoriented as she moved around. She finally recognized who Joaquin was and looked at D-Dog before she said, "Something smells awful."

Felix and I continued to fire our guns at the beasts. It reminded me of a carnival shooting gallery. Everything became murky at that point. I heard Joaquin yell for Felix; there was a gun exchanged, a scream, D-Dog barked, and then Joaquin was descending the steps, shooting his way down as Felix followed, carrying Theodora in outstretched arms. I hurried over to bring up the rear as we shot our way out of the pyramid room and scurried through one of the catwalk doors. We dashed through a dark, narrow corridor and found ourselves in a large underground cave. It was nothing like the narrow tunnel we had been in previously. This cave and the caves beyond were expansive, illuminated by fluorescent lights. I was able to bolt the door when we exited the pyramid room, but I was unsure of where we were.

I soon discovered what our location was; we had inadvertently stumbled straight into hell. We should have known better. Felix sat down on a boulder, and with Theodora draped across his lap, he let her sniff more of the *poción* from the countess. Joaquin sat down on a rock and freed D-Dog from the carpetbag. He ran up to me as I walked into the adjacent cave. I casually looked back and saw the Chupacabras. It rose, in an unfurling fashion, from the ground, behind Joaquin. Felix was right. There was no mistaking what it was. As it stood up, its shadow cast darkness across Joaquin's body. Joaquin was taking the bottle of water out of his bag when he became aware of the being's presence. I squatted down next to D-Dog and watched as Joaquin slowly raised his head and looked up over his shoulder. He didn't appear afraid, not yet. He appeared cautious, as if he didn't want to make any uncalculated moves. Joaquin slowly reached into his carpetbag and pulled his gun out. He held it close to his chest and flat across his heart. The Chupacabras raised its long arms into the air above Joaquin. Its nails were pointed like ice picks and its teeth were similarly pointed. It jerkily moved its body toward little Joaquin.

Joaquin fell backward, and as he did, his gun flew out of his hand and clattered on a rock before landing in the dirt. D-Dog attempted to race to him, but I grabbed him by his back leg and held on to him. Felix pushed Theodora up against the cave wall and stood in front of her. Kneeling, I held D-Dog with one hand and aimed my gun at the Chupacabras with the other. Across the tunnel Felix slowly turned his head and looked at me. The Chupacabras loomed over Joaquin. Its head turned in my direction. It breathed heavily and hissed at me and D-Dog. A spray of saliva issued from its mouth when it hissed. It turned and looked at Theodora and Felix, opened its mouth, and made a strange growling noise. Saliva dripped from its mouth. I could hear Joaquin quietly saying an Act of Contrition out loud. The Chupacabras snarled as it looked around the cave. Its head moved quickly from side to side, as if its neck had just been oiled.

I could very vaguely hear Joaquin repeat three times, "God, I don't want to die. God, I don't want to die. God, I don't want to die."

He had his hands clasped in front of him in prayer. His voice was shaky as he spoke. After all these years of friendship, I know Joaquin better than anyone else on earth. Little Joaquin was scared.

The Chupacabras raised its large arms over its head. It looked enormous in the cave. This was the moment. The Chupacabras was going to kill Joaquin in front of me—in front of all of us. As I cocked my pistol to shoot, a rumbling noise moved through the space.

I heard Joaquin say, "May God have mercy on my soul."

I was going to get one shot. One shot to save Joaquin's life. I aimed my gun and fired. It missed. Felix shot. He missed. The tunnel moved to the right and then it jerked to the left. I grabbed D-Dog and we were both thrown up against the wall. I couldn't see clearly. The tunnel filled with swirling dust. Everything was moving too quickly. I heard Theodora scream as large boulders fell from above. I watched as the wall beside me split open and a huge fissure was created before my eyes. I couldn't see Joaquin and I couldn't see the Chupacabras. A massive boulder blocked my view. The ground above us had opened up, and just like that, the sun's rays illuminated the cave.

In less than thirty seconds the shaking was over. It was another earthquake, and it had to be at least a 7.5 with the epicenter somewhere nearby. I knew I was alive and D-Dog was okay. I jumped up and raced to find the others.

Theodora and Felix apprehensively met me at the massive

boulder. There was no sign of Joaquin. The boulder occupied the space where he had lain reciting his Act of Contrition. The legs of the Chupacabras were visible; they stuck out from beneath the boulder. D-Dog sniffed the Chupacabras. I attempted to push the boulder but it wouldn't move. Felix and Theodora stared at me. Something didn't seem right. Joaquin wasn't under that huge rock. I knew that. I walked away, not wanting to look at them and not wanting them to see my face. I searched farther into the cave where the other rocks had fallen. Nothing; I found nothing. I looked up at the sun and followed its rays into the cave, walked to where the sun's rays ended, and searched in that area. It was there I found Joaquin wedged between a large boulder and the cave's wall. He didn't look dead, but he didn't look alive either. I yelled for Felix and he raced over. We lifted Joaquin up and carried him to where Theodora waited. Theodora and Felix stood behind me. They looked on but gave me some space.

I knelt down and said, "Joaquin, can you hear me?"

There was no answer. I took his hand in mine and patted it.

I repeated my words: "Joaquin, can you hear me?"

He did not answer.

D-Dog looked at him and made a small whimpering sound before he walked up and licked him on the cheek. Joaquin's head moved and his eyes opened. His eyes seemed unfocused until he saw and recognized D-Dog and me. He said one thing, and after he said that one thing, I knew everything was going to be okay.

While nodding, he said, "All that praying finally paid off."

Joaquin would later tell an amazing story that, while unbelievable, was still a story I wanted to believe. He said that as the Chupacabras stood over him he was sure his days on earth were about to end. Joaquin prayed to God for help as the animal snarled and looked about the cave at the rest of us. When the earthquake began, the Chupacabras moved closer toward him. As the beast bore down and was about to kill him Joaquin felt a force lift him up; his body moved through the cave's space but was guided by a hand that set him down where I found him. Joaquin claims it was then that the cave broke open and the massive boulder fell from above and onto the Chupacabras, crushing it. At that point Joaquin had looked in the direction of the sun, through the opening in the cave, but he didn't see it. In its place, he saw the All-Seeing Eye, or God's eye moving across the sky in a jerky motion. He felt faint and then blacked out until D-Dog licked him on the cheek.

Regarding the events that I have recounted as told to me by Joaquin, I logically and methodically deduced what could have happened. After I did that, I dismissed the logical and methodical explanation and instead have decided to believe the events as recounted by Joaquin for as long as we both shall live.

❖

We rested for a minute. Since Joaquin said he could walk and we all wanted to get away from the cave, we were able to improvise an exit and climb our way out because the ground had risen up alongside one wall. The shortcut was almost straight up but wasn't that high, maybe twelve feet. Felix went first. It was similar to rock climbing at a gym. It was merely a matter of finding the right steps and the right handholds. The only one who was slightly difficult to get to the top was Mr. D.

I climbed halfway up with him and raised him above my head. He sat in my hands as I lifted him up. Felix reached down from the top and pulled him up the rest of the way by gripping him under his front legs.

It took about half an hour, but when we had all assembled up on top we could see Cascada roughly a mile away. It stood alone upon a bluff with the Gulf of California as its watery backdrop. It had become windy and overcast. The wind blew through my clothes and dried some of the sweat on my body. It felt good. We stood under a cloudy landscape in the shadow of Don Humberto's fortress. The terrain consisted of desert plants, rocks, sand, weeds, dirt, sagebrush, and tumbleweeds. I looked around with what I'm sure could only be seen as disgust. All that was needed to give it the perfect finishing touch was a piece of trash and a cigarette butt. The landscape in the distance, at Cascada, was green and covered in vegetation. We all knew where we had to go. Nobody said a word. We looked at each other and, without any prompting, took off running in a mad scramble.

We had barely started out when it began to sprinkle. We ran through the landscape and I suspect we were all hoping to make it to Cascada before the downpour began. We did, and arrived relatively dry on the porch. Felix even had enough time to put the top up on his Impala before the real rain came. When it did, it was a thunderstorm.

We were leaving. We didn't talk about it. We didn't have to. There wasn't a need. This excursion was over, and we weren't going to ask for an extension on our lease. Theodora and Joaquin went upstairs to pack. After Felix finished attending to his car, he, too, went upstairs to gather his possessions. I stood on the porch with D-Dog watching the rain. Through the rain and lightning I saw Enrique and Rosa stumbling toward the house. They moved at a half-alive pace, faltering amongst the sagebrush and rocks; they would fall and drag themselves back to their feet to continue their journey. They were completely drenched and I couldn't think of a reason why they would be coming here. What could they possibly want? Shouldn't they be attending to Don Humberto or their ratty little Chupacabras friends? I kept an eye on them as they stumbled through the wet landscape. I noticed that each was carrying a rubber knapsack, which seemed peculiar. They continued to head toward the house, yet even though I tried to track their movements I still lost sight of them and they disappeared behind the house. I rushed down the steps to see where they had gone, but the relentless rain drove me back to the porch.

D-Dog and I raced into the house and ran to the kitchen so I could peer through the broken window. I searched through the dense rain but I couldn't see anything. D-Dog jumped about my feet and whined. He wanted me to pick him up, so I did and, in unison, we squinted our eyes and scanned the horizon for any sign of them.

I asked Mr. D., "Do you see anything?"

He looked at me and made that strange little dog noise which I took as a *no*, so I set him down on the floor and we walked out onto the back porch. We had no luck there either. Then D-Dog's ears went up, his head jerked to the side, and he took off. I raced after him to the doorless basement stoop. We cautiously walked down a few steps and found Rosa and Enrique.

Markie was not happy.

Those freakin' zombies were starting fires throughout the basement. I watched them pour gasoline, in a moderately focused way, over most of the boxes, yet half of the gasoline still ended up on the floor. They proceeded to light matches but not with any precision. It was all random and they enjoyed the flickering flames way too much. They would strike a match, gaze excitedly at its glow, throw it on a gasoline-soaked pile, and twirl. They twirled in a sulking, peculiar, depressed way. What kind of messed-up dancing is that? What kind of crazy crap is that? What kind of half-wit zombies are these two?

I demanded they *stop.*

I kept yelling, "Hey! Hey! Hey!" trying to attract their attention.

My gun was in its holster at my waist. I pulled it out and pointed it at them. I enjoyed holding it, but I couldn't shoot either, no matter how undead I believed them to be. What I really wanted to do was bitch-slap them, but bitch-slapping somebody with gasoline and matches probably isn't a very sane idea. Instead, I scooted my big male ass upstairs to enlist the aid of Felix and Joaquin, but those two, after all the killing we've done together, questioned what I had seen.

"Come and look," I said.

I motioned for them to follow, but they seemed to be humoring me.

I saw a slight smile on Felix's lips as Joaquin said, "Sure."

Joaquin was in the middle of packing until I reminded him I'd saved him from drowning. My exact words were, "You owe your life to me, so move your ass, Pepito…"

With absolute sincerity he looked me in the eyes and said, "I apologize for not taking you seriously." He continued, "If I remember right, you saved me the first time, and God saved me the second time."

At which point, he took off for the stairs. Felix grabbed his gun and followed.

By the time we made it to the basement's door stoop black

smoke was pluming through the cast-iron heating ducts on the first floor, hitting the ceiling in each room, and exploding into mushroom clouds. It had already gotten out of control in the short time it took me to run upstairs. We would never be able to stop this fire on our own. The black smoke gushing out of the basement doorway prevented us from going any farther.

We turned away from the smoke and it was then that Enrique the guitar man and Loca Rosa burst into the foyer and ran into the long adjoining parlor. Both of them were on fire but they didn't seem to care. Enrique sat down on the couch and Rosa wrapped herself in some of the drapes at the window. Felix moved quickly to do what I couldn't. He walked into the parlor and took care of Enrique first; he shot him in the side of the head. His brains splattered onto the upholstery before he slumped over onto the sofa. Then Felix walked over to Rosa, pointed his gun directly at her forehead, and she screamed. Her entire body was on fire and her face was covered in flames as she screamed a loud, horrendous Gates of Hell scream. Felix shot her in the forehead. She fell to the ground with a thud, pulling the burning curtains off their rod as she did so.

Joaquin turned around and raced up the foyer's staircase.

All he said in a frantic voice was, "D-Dog!"

Felix turned and followed him up the steps. I made my way into the parlor through the black smoke. I kept my hand over my nose and mouth and removed four Pre-Raphaelite paintings from the walls. I set them down on the foyer's floor, near the front door, then went back and attempted to put out the fire on the couch by hitting it with an oversized, fringed pillow. All I managed to do was catch the fringe on fire. The fire had moved into the realm of unstoppable. The house was doomed.

Within a minute, Joaquin came running down the steps.

D-Dog was on his leash, but Joaquin was carrying him. Joaquin had his hand over his nose and held Mr. D. close to his chest. Felix was behind him, and Theodora followed both of them in her quilted ceremonial robe, but she was twenty steps behind. Joaquin made it to the landing when that amazing technical marvel of a staircase began to first creak and break apart. The bottom steps broke free first and then each nail, each bolt, and each screw on each and every step from the bottom to the top popped in a domino effect. Theodora screamed as the top of the staircase fell in slow motion and the bottom of the staircase first rose slowly before the entire structure dropped down into the basement like a sinking ocean liner going to its grave. Both Felix and Theodora were suspended in the air for seconds before their own gravity pulled them down into the burning basement.

Joaquin, D-Dog, and I ran to the edge of the large hole, and the three of us peered down and tried to see through the smoke. None of us were going to survive much longer inside the house.

I told Joaquin, "Get on your hands and knees and get D-Dog outside." I pointed through the smoke at the paintings I could no longer see. "Grab those paintings over by the front door. Take them with you."

Joaquin looked at me, but didn't move. The look on his face was one of confusion.

"I'll meet you outside." I tried to nod reassuringly. "Go!"

Joaquin got down on his hands and knees. He held D-Dog's leash and the two moved slowly away from me into the black haze.

Through the dizzying smoke I could see Felix was up and walking, but Theodora appeared to be unconscious. She was sprawled motionless upon the steps. The staircase, while separated from the wall and floor, was still largely intact. Felix, wisely, was climbing from one step to the next to reach Theodora. The staircase was the only object in the basement not on fire. It was becoming even more difficult for me to breathe, so I lay flat upon the floor, belly to wood, and pulled my shirt up to cover my nose and mouth. Felix had reached Theodora and lifted her up. He carried her up the winding broken staircase toward me. The third-floor landing was now almost even with the foyer. I slid across the floor, closer to where Felix would emerge.

He carried Theodora up the twisted staircase structure with his arms extended in front of his body. She resembled a drowning victim. The ceremonial robe she wore was stark white compared to everything around her. Raging flames rose up from the basement. The flames crackled. Black smoke circled and attached itself to us. Felix lifted Theodora; I took her from him and pulled her alongside me. Felix crawled out of the large crater and scooped Theodora up into his arms. The long parlor, the home to all those undocumented paintings, was engulfed in flames. We hurriedly evacuated the house as explosions burst throughout the structure and windows blew out. Flames climbed out of the windows and crawled up the side of the building. We raced to Felix's Impala parked on the grass.

It was then that the rain stopped.

All I was able to save, beside my camera, were some large sunglasses, the serape poncho, and my oversized sombrero, and only because they were in the Impala's trunk. Felix laid Theodora down on the green grass. He knelt down by her side, shielding her face from the last drops of rain. She opened her eyes slowly, as if she had been in a long slumber.

She looked up at Felix De La Santos and said, "You're always saving my life."

Felix smiled. He bent down and kissed her. It was quite unexpected. I didn't see *that* coming.

I elbowed Joaquin in the side and spoke through smiling teeth like a ventriloquist. "Did you know?"

Joaquin shook his head in the negative right before Theodora whispered to Felix in a dreamy, half-awake way, "Take my hand?"

She put her hand in his.

Joaquin tapped me on the shoulder and said in a hushed tone, "Let's give them some privacy."

He motioned with his finger for me to follow him. He led me across the manicured lawn to an overgrown bougainvillea vine with pink and white flowers; in front of it stood a jacaranda tree. He crouched down next to the jacaranda, reached behind it, and grabbed something.

He looked at me and said, "I was only able to rescue one painting because that's all I could find in the smoke."

I was hoping for four, but I'm not overly greedy.

"What? What were you able to rescue?" I asked with some trepidation, trying not to get my hopes up.

He pulled from behind the tree a Holman Hunt painting he had hidden under some large rubber tree leaves. It was the painting of a woman in a white robe floating in a lake surrounded by reeds and a marsh. Her eyes are closed and it's unclear if she's dead or alive. It was very reminiscent of John Everett Millais's *Ophelia*. Joaquin held the framed painting up in front of me, hiding his face behind it.

"There's no title for the painting on the back or the front," he said.

He turned it around so I could examine the back, but he still hid his face behind the canvas.

"Since it's never been documented, can we name it?" he asked.

I looked at the back of the painting while I pondered the issue. "What a perplexing question," I said, and looked back at Felix and Theodora. "You wouldn't see that as jumping the gun?"

Joaquin did not respond.

I took the painting from him and held it up in front of myself. After contemplating it for a moment, I said, "There's only one appropriate name. Don't you think?"

Joaquin came out from behind the painting and seemed to be staring at my ear. He's such a little weirdo.

"Uh, the painting is over here," I said as I held it with one hand and pointed at it with the other.

Joaquin looked at the painting with one eye closed and one eye opened. This is the way he looked at me when he said, "So from this day forward..." He stopped.

I began where he left off. "We'll call it *The Bride of the Chupacabras*."

The next day Theodora and Felix were married by a justice of the peace in downtown San Felipe; Joaquin, D-Dog, and I were their only guests. We both wanted to be Felix's best man, so there was a great deal of pushing and shoving by that little weasel Joaquin and for the likes of me, I swear, I never pushed him even though he fibbed and said I did. It finally got so bad that Felix pointed at D-Dog and said he was going to be "best dog," at which point he clipped the wedding rings to D-Dog's cape with a safety pin. Uh, I suggested Joaquin be the maid of honor, but he gave me *a look* and declined. I also think he gave me the finger when I wasn't looking. I'm not sure, but I know I saw something.

Theodora wouldn't think of wearing anything but the white ceremonial robe with quilted collar and cuffs as her wedding dress.

She said, "I was almost killed in it. I was kept captive in it, and I was rescued in it. I might as well get married in it."

All her other clothes had burned up in the fire, so it actually made logical sense, too.

❖

Their reception included Joaquin and me as guests. There was also one dog (uh, D-Dog). It was held at the Americano Cantina in downtown San Felipe. The Americano caters to the American tourist trade by having a jukebox with a wide selection of American music. For the celebration I wore my serape poncho and my oversized sombrero. Joaquin was still in his crisscross of symbols, and Theodora wore her quilted wedding dress. Only Felix dressed normally. Joaquin and I bought him a cowboy hat as a wedding gift, which he wore, along with his holster and gun set, adding an outlaw vibe to the proceedings.

Since it was an afternoon shindig, the place was practically empty and we had the cantina to ourselves. The newlyweds' first dance together was to a jazzy song from the 1950s. Theodora selected it. After a couple of drinks, and because I'm a graduate of the Golden Shoehorn Academy of Dance, I persuaded everybody to line up and attempted to teach them the Macarena. Hey, it was on the jukebox. After a minute of instruction Theodora could have taken over as instructor, and surprisingly, Felix could not only follow instructions but could bust a move, too. We danced with me out in front and the three of them behind me. In the mirrors that lined the walls opposite us I could see everyone's dancing ability; oh Lordy, my Lordy. We looked good. Naturally, I incorporated some personal flourishes into my routine; an extra head turn, a long sexy look, and some over-the-top, manly booty movement. After that I entertained everybody for thirty seconds or less when I stuck my thumbs in my belt and did a hillbilly jig. Shuffling in my poncho and sombrero made me look like a Mexican *heel-bill-y*.

Theodora wanted to vogue to that "Vogue" song, so I suddenly had to channel the male model within me. Felix and Joaquin immediately saw what kind of a fierce competition Theodora and I would be locked in, so they both sat down to watch. I could have won, I could have out-danced Theodora, but I got overambitious with some ill-thought-out tumbling moves that were supposed to culminate in a classy breakdance spinning finale. The tumbling went fine at first. I was like a big metal drum, flopping over, flopping over, flopping over, flopping over. Unfortunately, my serape poncho got stuck over my head while I was tumbling. I became confused and almost rolled over Mr. D. who, for some reason, was jumping around right next to me and barking as I tumbled. He took off like a jackrabbit when I started spinning, but I was flailing around so uncouthly that I aborted that move and jumped up. When I got back to my feet I was so dizzy I was vogueing in a rhythmless, woozy, gringo way. My arms were up and away from my body with my palms out. I rocked from side to side, shifting my weight from one foot to the other. I was a dancing bear trying to keep my opponent at bay. I attempted to do some fancy, spacetastic moonwalking but my feet got tangled up, I slipped and fell right on my big man butt, which completely ended the dance-off. The verdict: I lost due to overt clumsiness and lack of poise. When I looked at D-Dog, he opened his eyes wide and made that strange little dog noise before he sheepishly looked away.

When the dog is embarrassed by my actions, I know I've made a fool of myself.

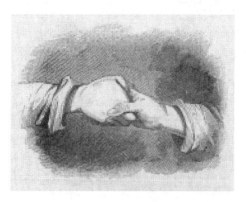

XI.
Mark Crowden's Blog: Three Days Later

We were sitting in a turn-out on the highway headed back to the US. Felix and Theodora sat in the front seat of the '67 Impala. I sat in the backseat behind Felix who, of course, was driving, and Joaquin sat across from me with D-Dog. D-Dog was still wearing his cape, and Joaquin continued to wear his crisscross of symbols. He kept wearing it because "it brought him good luck." I didn't want to tell him but it was starting to smell. I put on my California Raisin sunglasses I had thankfully packed for our excursion to Mexico. True, they were oversized, bordering on crazy big, but they had great memories attached to them from a Halloween years ago when I dressed up as a raisin along with some friends. I was also wearing my oversized sombrero and poncho.

Theodora had a cigarette hanging from her lip as she turned back and stared at me.

"What?" I asked.

"Are you going to give him the present?"

D-Dog and Joaquin looked from Theodora to me. I was in charge of the present. I was hiding it under my sombrero. I took off my sombrero, felt around on the top of my head for a small box, located it, hid it in my big hand, and put my sombrero back on. I told Joaquin to close his eyes and hold out his hand. Felix and Theodora looked on. I put a small white box wrapped and tied with red ribbon in Joaquin's palm. D-Dog sniffed it.

"You can open your eyes," I said.

"What is it?" Joaquin asked.

"It's an early Christmas present." I pointed at Theodora and Felix. "We all pitched in to buy it. D-Dog picked out the ribbon."

Joaquin untied the ribbon and placed it on D-Dog's head so the ends hung like pigtails along his dog face. He opened the small white box, which contained a small silver pin of the All-Seeing Eye. The eye was silver with black enamel. The rays emanating from the eye were tooled silver sticks in various lengths.

"We had it made for you," I said.

Joaquin removed it from the box and looked at it.

I continued, "It's kind of like a brooch. I know that's a girl thing, but you're man enough to pull it off."

I took it from him and pinned it on his crisscross of symbols. I patted it down and said, "There. It looks great."

Felix gave Joaquin a thumbs-up and Theodora smiled as she blew some cigarette smoke in his direction.

Joaquin started to get teary-eyed, so I asked, "Are you okay?"

He nodded.

"Are you happy?"

He nodded again.

"Then why are you going to cry?" I asked.

Joaquin looked at Theodora, Felix, D-Dog, and me before saying, "Because I finally have the family I've always wanted."

I couldn't let anyone see how his confession affected me, so I quickly turned away and looked out the window. His words bit into my heart. I'll have to have it checked for teeth marks now. I knew the four of them were waiting for a response. I took off my sunglasses and turned back to Joaquin. He had pulled his crisscross of symbols away from his chest and was looking down at this new pin. He raised his head to look at me. I stared at him for the longest time before I snorted. Upon his chest God's eye sparkled in the sunlight. It made me rethink my behavior. I certainly didn't want to get on God's wrong side, so as self-imposed penance I reached out and rubbed Joaquin's head with my hand. The response I received from him was a silent look followed by a blink. D-Dog wasn't as sedate. He wrangled one end of the ribbon that decorated his head into his mouth by turning his head to the side and repeatedly biting the air until he got it between his lips. He was now nibbling on the ribbon while he looked up at me.

Family; he saw me as family. Well, the idea doesn't make me shudder. I should have known that was our destination all along. I certainly don't want the last line in my obit to read, *There are no immediate survivors.* Joaquin claims that's the saddest line to stumble across in a newspaper obituary. I've never agreed with him, but he might be right.

The Odd Fellow in me compelled me to do the right thing and offer my hand in solidarity and friendship. Joaquin looked at my hand; its whiteness shook slightly in front of all of us and revealed that my bravery barely made it past my wrist. As Joaquin reached out and grasped my hand, I realized that the tenets of friendship, love, and truth would bind us together from this day forward. Theodora and Felix nodded as our hands shook together under God's watchful eye. It was then, when I had finally come to terms with the direction of my life, that Felix stepped on the gas and that 1967 Chevy Impala sped out onto the highway.

About the Author

Guillermo Luna enjoys staying at home and watching his favorite reality TV shows. One of his present goals is to watch all the movies he hasn't seen, and he has a soft spot for film noir. On the weekends, he's usually driving around looking for great buys at flea markets and antique stores. He has an undergraduate degree in journalism and two master's degrees—one in cinema and the other in library science, which is quite a feat for someone who sees himself as an underachiever. When he's not listening to *The Lark Ascending* or "Clair de Lune," he's listening to music from the '60s and '70s. He's single and can't envision having another roommate but would consider a cat or dog. He takes public transportation to work, which affords him the free time to read the *Los Angeles Times* every morning. He's a supervisor in a university library.

Books Available From Bold Strokes Books

In Between by Jane Hoppen. At the age of 14, Sophie Schmidt discovers that she was born an intersexual baby and sets off on a journey to find her place in a world that denies her true existence. (978-1-60282-968-8)

The Odd Fellows by Guillermo Luna. Joaquin Moreno and Mark Crowden open a bed-and-breakfast in Mexico but soon must confront an evil force with only friendship, love, and truth as their weapons. (978-1-60282-969-5)

The Seventh Pleiade by Andrew J. Peters. When Atlantis is besieged by violent storms, tremors, and a barbarian army, it will be up to a young gay prince to find a way for the kingdom's survival. (978-1-60282-960-2)

Cutie Pie Must Die by R.W. Clinger. Sexy detectives, a muscled quarterback, and the queerest murders…when murder is most cute. (978-1-60282-961-9)

Going Down for the Count by Cage Thunder. Desperately needing money, Gary Harper answers an ad that leads him into the underground world of gay professional wrestling—which leads him on a journey of self-discovery and romance. (978-1-60282-962-6)

Light by 'Nathan Burgoine. Openly gay (and secretly psychokinetic) Kieran Quinn is forced into action when self-styled prophet Wyatt Jackson arrives during Pride Week and things take a violent turn. (978-1-60282-953-4)

Baton Rouge Bingo by Greg Herren. The murder of an animal rights activist involves Scotty and the boys in a decades-old mystery revolving around Huey Long's murder and a missing fortune. (978-1-60282-954-1)

Anything for a Dollar, edited by Todd Gregory. Bodies for hire, bodies for sale—enter the steaming hot world of men who make a living from their bodies—whether they star in porn, model, strip, or hustle—or all of the above. (978-1-60282-955-8)

Mind Fields by Dylan Madrid. When college student Adam Parsh accepts a tutoring position, he finds himself the object of the dangerous desires of one of the most powerful men in the world—his married employer. (978-1-60282-945-9)

Greg Honey by Russ Gregory. Detective Greg Honey is steering his way through new love, business failure, and bruises when all his cases indicate trouble brewing for his wealthy family. (978-1-60282-946-6)

Lake Thirteen by Greg Herren. A visit to an old cemetery seems like fun to a group of five teenagers, who soon learn that sometimes it's best to leave old ghosts alone. (978-1-60282-894-0)

Deadly Cult by Joel Gomez-Dossi. One nation under MY God, or you die. (978-1-60282-895-7)

The Case of the Rising Star: A Derrick Steele Mystery by Zavo. Derrick Steele's next case involves blackmail, revenge, and a new romance as Derrick races to save a young movie star from a dangerous killer. Meanwhile, will a new threat from within destroy him, along with the entire Steele family? (978-1-60282-888-9)

Big Bad Wolf by Logan Zachary. After a wolf attack, Paavo Wolfe begins to suspect one of the victims is turning into a werewolf. Things become hairy as his ex-partner helps him find the killer. Can Paavo solve the mystery before he runs into the Big Bad Wolf? (978-1-60282-890-2)

The Moon's Deep Circle by David Holly. Tip Trencher wants to find out what happened to his long-lost brothers, but what he finds is a sizzling circle of gay sex and pagan ritual. (978-1-60282-870-4)

The Plain of Bitter Honey by Alan Chin. Trapped within the bleak prospect of a society in chaos, twin brothers Aaron and Hayden Swann discover inner strength in the face of tragedy and search for atonement after betraying the one you most love. (978-1-60282-883-4)

Tricks of the Trade: Magical Gay Erotica, edited by Jerry L. Wheeler. Today's hottest erotica writers take you inside the sultry, seductive world of magicians and their tricks—professional and otherwise. (978-1-60282-781-3)

Straight Boy Roommate by Kevin Troughton. Tom isn't expecting much from his first term at University, but a chance encounter with straight boy Dan catapults him into an extraordinary, wild weekend of sex and self-discovery, which turns his life upside down, and leads him into his first love affair. (978-1-60282-782-0)

In His Secret Life by Mel Bossa. The only man Allan wants is the one he can't have. (978-1-60282-875-9)

Promises in Every Star, edited by Todd Gregory. Acclaimed gay erotica author Todd Gregory's definitive collection of short stories, including both classic and new works. (978-1-60282-787-5)

Raising Hell: Demonic Gay Erotica, edited by Todd Gregory. Hot stories of gay erotica featuring demons. (978-1-60282-768-4)

Pursued by Joel Gomez-Dossi. Openly gay college student Jamie Bradford becomes romantically involved with two men at the same time, and his hell begins when one of his boyfriends becomes intent on killing him. (978-1-60282-769-1)

Timothy by Greg Herren. *Timothy* is a romantic suspense thriller from award-winning mystery writer Greg Herren set in the fabulous Hamptons. (978-1-60282-760-8)

In Stone by Jeremy Jordan King. A young New Yorker is rescued from a hate crime by a mysterious someone who turns out to be more of a something. (978-1-60282-761-5)

Combustion by Daniel W. Kelly. Bearish detective Deck Waxer comes to the city of Kremfort Cove to investigate why the hottest men in town are bursting into flames in broad daylight. (978-1-60282-763-9)

Strange Bedfellows by Rob Byrnes. Partners in life and crime, Grant Lambert and Chase LaMarca are hired to make a politician's compromising photo disappear, but what should be an easy job quickly spins out of control. (978-1-60282-746-2)

The Jesus Injection by Eric Andrews-Katz. Murderous statues, demented drag queens, political bombings, ex-gay ministries, espionage, and romance are all in a day's work for a top secret agent. But the gloves are off when Agent Buck 98 comes up against the Jesus Injection. (978-1-60282-762-2)

Night Shadows: Queer Horror edited by Greg Herren and J.M. Redmann. *Night Shadows* features delightfully wicked stories by some of the biggest names in queer publishing. (978-1-60282-751-6)

Secret Societies by William Holden. An outcast hustler, his unlikely "mother," his faithless lovers, and his religious persecutors—all in 1726. (978-1-60282-752-3)

The Jetsetters by David-Matthew Barnes. As rock band the Jetsetters skyrocket from obscurity to superstardom, Justin Holt, a lonely barista, and Diego Delgado, the band's guitarist, fight with everything they have to stay together, despite the chaos and fame. (978-1-60282-745-5)

The Dirty Diner: Gay Erotica on the Menu, edited by Jerry L. Wheeler. Gay erotica set in restaurants, featuring food, sex, and men—could you really ask for anything more? (978-1-60282-677-9)

Sweat: Gay Jock Erotica by Todd Gregory. Sizzling tales of smoking-hot sex with the athletic studs everyone fantasizes about. (978-1-60282-669-4)

The Marrying Kind by Ken O'Neill. Just when successful wedding planner Adam More decides to protest inequality by quitting the business and boycotting marriage entirely, his only sibling announces her engagement. (978-1-60282-670-0)